Mary Hallock Foote

The Last Assembly Ball

And, the fate of a voice

Mary Hallock Foote

The Last Assembly Ball
And, the fate of a voice

ISBN/EAN: 9783337105761

Printed in Europe, USA, Canada, Australia, Japan

Cover: Foto ©Andreas Hilbeck / pixelio.de

More available books at **www.hansebooks.com**

THE LAST ASSEMBLY BALL

AND

THE FATE OF A VOICE

BY

MARY HALLOCK FOOTE

AUTHOR OF "THE LED-HORSE CLAIM" AND "JOHN BODEWIN'S
TESTIMONY"

BOSTON AND NEW YORK
HOUGHTON, MIFFLIN AND COMPANY
The Riverside Press, Cambridge
1889

The Riverside Press, Cambridge, Mass., U. S. A.
Electrotyped and Printed by H. O. Houghton & Co.

CONTENTS.

THE LAST ASSEMBLY BALL.

INTRODUCTORY.

THE East generalizes the West much as
England has the habit of generalizing Amer-
ica; taking note of picturesque outward differences, easily perceived across a breadth of
continent. Among other unsafe assump-
tions, the East has decided that nothing can
be freer and simpler than the social life of
the far West, exemplified by the flannel
shirt and the flowing necktie, the absence of
polish on boots and manners.

But as a matter of experience, no society
is so puzzling in its relations, so exacting in
its demands upon self-restraint, as one which
has no methods, which is yet in the stage of
fermentation. Middle age has decided, or
has learned to dispense with, many things
which youth continues to fash itself about;

and the older societies, with all their perpetuated grooves and deep-rooted complexities, are freer and more cheerful than the new.

In constructing a pioneer community one must add to the native, Western-born element, the "tenderfoot" element, so called, — self-conscious, new to surrounding standards, warped by disappointment or excited by success, torn, femininely speaking, between a past not yet abandoned and a present reluctantly accepted. Add, generally, the want of homogeneity in a population hastily recruited from divers States, cities, nationalities, with a surplus of youth, energy, incapacity, or misfortune to dispose of; add the melancholy of a land oppressed by too much nature, — not mother nature of the Christian poets, but nature of the dark old mythologies, — the spectacle of a creation indeed scarcely more than six days old. When Adam's celestial visitor (in the seventh book of Paradise Lost) condescends to relate how the world was first created, he gives an astonishing picture of the sixth and last great act; when the earth brought forth the living creature after its kind regardless of zones and habitudes, crawling, wriggling, pawing from the sod, rent to favor the transmission. Life on the surface could not have been simple, for a few days at least, after that violent and promiscuous birth.

The life of the West historically, like the story of Man, is an epic, a song tale of grand meanings. Socially, it is a genesis, a formless record of beginnings, tragic, grotesque, sorrowful, unrelated, except as illustrations of a tendency towards confusion and failure, with contrasting lights of character, and high personal achievement. The only successful characterizations of it in literature have treated it in this episodic manner.

But looking forward to the story in periods, the West has a future, socially, of enormous promise. It has all the elements of greatness, when it shall have passed the period of uncouth strivings, and that later stage of material satisfaction which is the sequel to the age of force. The East denies it modesty, but there is a humility that apes pride as well as a pride that apes humility. It has never been denied generosity, charity, devotedness, humor of a peculiarly effective quality, a desire for self-improvement, unconquerable, often pathetic, courage, and enthusiasm. It has that admixture of contrasting national types which gives us the golden thread of genius. Finally, the New South is seeking its future there — not a future of conquest, but of patience and hard work.

The West is not to be measured by homesick tales from an Eastern point of view. The true note will be struck when the alien touch no longer blunts the chord, groping for futile harmonies, through morbid minor strains; when we have our novelists of the Pacific slope, cosmopolite by blood, acclimated through more than one generation to the heady air of the plains, bred in the traditions of an older civilization — or, better still, with a wild note as frank as that which comes to us from the sad northern steppe.

PART I.

THE SITUATION.

I.

THE overland train which took westward, in the fall of 1879, Francis Embury, aged twenty-four, swung along to the rhythm of certain well-strummed stanzas that sang in the young man's head with as genuine, passionate iteration as once they must have beat in the brain of the poet.

O my cousin, shallow-hearted! O my Amy, mine no more!

We, whose pretty girl cousins are getting to be middle-aged ladies, and who have ceased to shiver at the sounding metres of Locksley Hall, may smile at these words, but they had tingling meanings for the cousin of Miss Catherine Mason of Mamaroneck, in the county of Westchester.

O the dreary, dreary moorland! O the barren, barren shore!

We know there are no moorlands about Mamaroneck; but moorlands or marsh-lands, Amy or Catherine, the train clanked on, indifferent to the new burden or the old, and as to the dreariness and the barrenness and the shallow-heartedness, nothing need be conceded on the score of youthful wretchedness.

But it would have been going too far, even for the sake of putting her more in the wrong, to have insisted that Catherine Mason was to be "mated with a clown." The clown of Westchester County, whatever may be the nature of him, has no attractions that we know of for the parents of pretty cousins, nor were Mr. and Mrs. Ennis Mason at all likely to bestir themselves in the matter of a marriage connection for their daughter. It was only in a negative way that they concerned themselves, and, as their disaffected young relative bitterly reflected, where the claimant was of their own blood.

The difficulty itself was a despairingly simple one. Eleanor Mason, Catherine's elder sister, had married her first cousin, after a good deal of quiet but exceedingly earnest discussion, which had gone on over the heads of the younger members of the family. Francis Embury was not a first cousin, but when his turn came Mrs. Mason had declared, without any discussion, that she desired no more cousins in her family, whether once or twice removed, in the capacity of sons-in-law. Her husband was effectually of the same mind, and the Emburys, father and mother, were not behind in their objections.

It might have been urged that Eleanor's marriage, having proved a happy one with all the usual blessings — and some that were unusual — upon it, should have supplied a family precedent, but the parents on both sides illogically refused to consider it as such. They talked with their children apart, and in these conferences strange lights were thrown upon the family history, a branch of research young people are usually indifferent to until they become heads of families themselves, and begin to look for tendencies in their children, or excuses for the same when found. Old seals of silence were broken; records, which the elders of the family keep, like sibylline books, closed against the day of doubt and confusion, were consulted, and the sky of youth, painted with rosy dreams, showed portents which the fathers and mothers spared not to interpret with prophetic plainness.

The young man was wild — against his parents, against her parents, against the girl herself, who faltered and sickened and gave up her hope.

She swept up the bangs from her fair forehead, which was over high for such strenuous treatment, and clung more than ever to the mother who, with pain not less than her own, had dealt her the blow.   It is the nature of some girls to be "servile" in this way, as it is the nature of the young men who suffer from their want of spirit to call them cold, characterless, shallow-hearted — "puppets," in short.

Catherine's conduct, it must be confessed, was not in the spirit of her time and her country ; she would not declare for happiness and her lover.   The family verdict prevailed, and Frank Embury hurled himself across the continent by the first train westward.

The great mining boom of 1879–80 was then in the ascendant.   No doubt many of the young men who joined the stampede for Leadville at this time went, like Frank, under conviction of the worthlessness of all that remained to them of life, especially the feminine portion of it, and were the more inclined to be reckless in their bids for that ironical species of fortune which is said to perch upon the banner of love, at half-mast.

A concussion of the heart, at a time when the circulation is restoratively active, has pitched many a good husband and useful citizen safely into the midst of a prosperous career; but an average result in these cases must be difficult to arrive at so long as the publicity of the experiment depends upon its success. The failures go down upon private records, not easily traced or verified. In the case of Frank Embury nothing worse seemed likely to come of his mishap, his parents flattered themselves, than a little timely attention to business in a direction hitherto distasteful to the young man. He remembered that he had a profession — adopted to please his family and coquetted with since, on various pretexts satisfactory to no one but himself. He did not know, perhaps, that there were already in the camp upwards of twenty graduates of the Columbia School of Mines alone, besides representatives of every other institution in the country which has the honor of producing a yearly crop of civil or mining engineers.   But if he had known it, it is not probable the fact would have deterred him from projecting himself upon his fate.   The malcontents of all kinds inevitably go West, if they are young and not well provided with this world's goods.

Frank lighted upon his feet in one of those communities which are proverbially engaged in burning the candle at both ends. Here were no fathers and mothers of an age to balk youth of the courage of its impulses. Men not much older than himself gave the tone in society and in business; rushed into alliances, offensive and defensive; declared war and laughed in each other's faces over their shot-guns.   Life and death were lightly held compared with questions affecting the egoism of youth, its rights and privileges, its haughty immunities.   Social knots, which have been patiently picked at for generations, these jaunty civic fathers disposed of at a blow.

Across the continent, clans and families looked on aghast as the spindle whirled and the thread of these tense young lives was swiftly spun; and the shears, which in older communities are wont to creak a little and give a poor moment's warning, were ready with their work.

Embury arrived, in time to dispute with an older graduate of his own college the ominous distinction of thirteenth assayer in the camp. The young men concluded to divide the objectionable number between them, and each became the twelfth and a half. The sign of Williams and Embury invited patronage as assayers of metals or as experts in the examination of mines; though it may be assumed that in the latter capacity the experience of both young partners put together could have been but an expensive sort of guesswork, for those who employed it.

The town was in a state of chaotic expansion, with throes of laughter at its own unwieldiness. It was difficult to get enough to eat, impossible to find a decent place to eat it in. Ancient deplorable jokes about the "Forty-niners," who slept in barrels at five dollars a night, with their feet outside, were revived with childish appreciation of their humor. Soft-handed youths, fresh from Eastern colleges and ball-rooms, found themselves twirling frying-pans as familiarly as if they had been pretty girls' fans or favors in a german, and better than a rose in a button-hole was the button itself, when it could be relied upon not to come off.

The Clarendon Hotel was then building; the Windsor had not been projected. Ranks of men in triple file lined the counters in every eating-shop, — tables and chairs were as yet not thought of, — laughing, shoving, gesticulating, endeavoring by bribes and curses to influence the impartial tide of bad victuals steaming in from the reeking kitch- ens. Much time as well as temper was lost in these periodic struggles, and the food when captured was execrable. Our two young men therefore adopted a mode of life then common in the camp, called "baching it," in the two bare rooms they had striven for with several other applicants, before the roof was over them.

Frank, who had no gift for cooking, was unable to dispute his manifest destiny as dishwasher. It was he, therefore, who first tired of the mutual housekeeping, and who roamed the town, every hour he could spare for research, in the hope of finding the com-

ing woman. Chinese labor had been excluded from this camp of idealists, yet the
demand for white labor had not created the
supply; there was dearth of woman's cooking, — and eke of woman's dishwashing,
thought poor Frank.

About this time a gleam of hope came to
him from the "Tent Bakery," as it was
called, where, in the white photographic light
of a canvas roof, bread and pastry could be
bought which had the home-made flavor. He
induced Williams to throw aside his skillets
and saucepans, and the pair took home
schoolboy meals in paper-bags, subsisting
upon buns and canned meats and wearying
for the taste of a hot broiled steak. They
agreed that this state of things could not last,
watching hungrily meanwhile the progress
of the new hotel, which filled an entire block
of Harrison Avenue with ample promise of
hospitality.

In the mean time there had come to the
camp an intrepid little widow of — let us say
Denver, not to be personal. She was a woman of a practical turn, which did not pre-
vent her from being decidedly pretty. Mrs.
Fanny Dansken had not been slow to per-

ceive the advantages of the new camp as a place wherein to make a little money quickly in a way she had thought of, and to invest it — with what chances who could say? Her way of making money was a very simple one. For most women, and under the usual circumstances, there are few ways that are harder; but Mrs. Dansken purposed to reverse the usual anxious order of things in the business of taking boarders, and instead of seeking, allow herself to be sought. In that homeless, hungry, distraught community of men she had reason to believe that her experiment would be unique.

She took a high tone from the beginning, a comically lofty one, considering her resources; but she was careful that no one but the author of the situation should see the fun of it. She trusted to be able to hold her own until she could afford, financially speaking, to ship her oars and spread her sails to the rising gale that was humming through the stock market, from Wall Street to the Golden Gate. Then it would be time enough to share the joke.

She opened her house on Harrison Avenue, on the west side, a few blocks above the skel-

eton stories of her formidable rival, the Clarendon. No. 9 had the usual square board
front, thinly painted, the new pine showing
with cold pinkness through a scumbling of
white lead. To the original four-room cabin
she had caused to be added a long extension,
running back into the lot in which the house
stood alone. From the kitchen door a path
led out upon some vague, parallel street,
where the buildings as yet were too far apart
to obstruct the prospect across such a hag-
gard stretch of country as made the new tenant homesick to look at, although she was not
an imaginative person, and for many years
had called no place in particular her home.
Beyond were the mountains, giving perpetual
emphasis to the human achievement; for
every item of manufactured material that
had gone to the building and plenishing of
this gaunt, growthy young settlement, every
circumstance that contributed to its insatiate
life, from the piano in its dance-halls to the
shards and rags on its dust-heaps, had come
over those sternly unimplicated mountains,
by ways needless to describe to those who are
familiar with such ways, and impossible to
those who are not. The journey in itself

constituted an understood bond among the citizens. Each knew how the others had got there, and could guess, within limits, why they had come. It was not for their health, they gayly admitted, looking about them at those bony foster-mothers, Breece and Freyer and Carbonate Hills.

Mrs. Dansken found, as she had anticipated, that in making up the tale of her guests she could take her pick of the town. The process of selection was necessarily a hasty one; but, considering the place, she made very few mistakes. It was understood that a seat at her table was to be well paid for, outside of the privilege itself. She was perhaps lucky in her first applicants; these implied others of the same sort. Very soon a company of sunburned faces that would have been presentable anywhere, met nightly in the light of the crimson silk-shaded lamp, the sun and centre of Mrs. Dansken's dinner-table.

It is laughable, it is pitiful, to remember how little it took to create something like an environment in that home of the self-exiled. A lamp with a soft lustre; a pretty little stranger woman at the head of a table, spread with clear glass and spotless linen and the best an inchoate market could afford ; chairs that stood upon four legs without wobbling ; good health, youthful appetites, not too much knowledge of each other ; distant homes and loves and friends in the background, to whom all this strangeness was tenderly referred. Outside, the shrill air of the spring twilight at an altitude of eleven thousand feet above the level of the sea ; six inches of snow on the board sidewalks, mountains whiter than the clouds, and black with patches of burnt forest ; smoke of smelters languidly rising ; voices and footsteps, all of strangers ; over all an atmosphere of insensate gayety, of fantastic success.

II.

MRS. DANSKEN stood in the path behind her kitchen door one morning, watching across the street the funeral of a well-known " jumper," who had been shot in a quarrel over a piece of disputed land. The poor cabin could not contain the new-made widow's grief. She was crying, bare-headed, in the bleak noon sunlight, while her husband's confrères, in Masonic bibs and aprons, were shouldering the coffin into the plumed hearse. The children of the neighborhood had gathered to the spectacle, and followed as it moved down the street with throbbing of drums, wailing of fifes, and buzzing of brass. The widow and her brood had been bundled into the carriage magnificently provided by charity, at a cost that would have fed them for a month. They sat in it charily, in their shabby weeds, eying its soiled upholstery with an awe which even the freshness of their grief could not blunt.

Mrs. Dansken buried her face in her apron and laughed, hysterically. Looking up, she saw a young man at the gate, studying the house as if to reassure himself of his locality. He beamed, hat in hand, at the sight of her brightly illumined figure in the sunny path; perhaps with relief that she had not, as he had at first supposed, been crying.

"Is this No. 9?" he inquired. "I seem to have come out on the wrong street."

"Yes, our front door is on Harrison Avenue; but it does n't matter. Will you come in?"

"Is this Mrs. Dansken? I 'm sure it is!'"
He smiled down at the shining brown head
and white lawn apron, tied in a bow in front
of a neat waist.

Mrs. Dansken laughed. "Then I need not
say that it is, if you are sure." They were
skirting the kitchen regions towards the front
door.

"I hope you 'll forgive me for insisting
that you 're Mrs. Dansken, but I 'm so awfully anxious to know if you will have room
for us, — my partner and me."

"Yes, perhaps, when I know who you are.
You know there are a great many of you."

"And only one of you, unfortunately."

This was the way Mrs. Dansken liked to be
approached. She looked the new applicant
over in the shade of her doorway. He was
extremely good-looking, so far as that went;
but Mrs. Dansken did not choose her boarders for their bright eyes or for the number
of inches they stood in their boots. She
let this one produce his credentials, beginning with his name, Mr. Francis Embury,
No. 174 of a respectable-sounding street,
with New York added in pencil, on the card
he gave her. Of his partner, Hugh Wil-

liams, she already knew something; indeed, young Embury was not altogether a stranger tó her, as she allowed him to suppose, while she sat calmly considering his proposal. If she understood her part in the negotiation, it was plain to her that he was by no means unpracticed in his. But in this she was mistaken: Frank was simply one of these charming young fellows to whom the art of coaxing comes by nature, but who are found to be exceedingly obstinate when the same sort of pressure is applied to themselves.

She smiled at him, out of her narrow shining eyes, with merry little creases at the corners. He was gayly insistent. He proposed to present himself with his partner at dinner that same evening. They were famished, he declared. They had been living upon husks, and had done nothing to deserve it.

Mrs. Dansken could only promise them a very small portion of a fatted calf, she said, if they were resolved upon coming that night; and then she coyly mentioned sweet-breads, at which the young fellow fairly howled with delight, so that it was impossible to help laughing. They laughed together, like old acquaintances, and the business was settled.

Mrs. Dansken was in the habit of shar-
ing her news, if it was good news, with her
silent partner in the kitchen, Ann Matthews,
an old servant of her mother's whom she
had imported at considerable expense, with
a far-sighted eye to the foundations of success in a camp without a cuisine.

Ann's excellent skill in cooking was a
gift which had upheld its possessor in the
darkest hours of a somewhat morose dispo-
sition. In these moods she could absorb flat-
tery as a black garment gathers the rays
of the sun, and Mrs. Dansken gave it her
in the universal belief in the efficacy of this
simple remedy ; though Ann, unlike the traveler in the fable, clung to her cloak long after she was warmed through and through.
Ann would have been called a " far-downer "
by her lively countrymen from Cork ; but
she gloried in having " come from the
County Tyrone, among the green bushes,"
and if her lips had ever been intimate with
the Blarney Stone the spell, upon her caustic
tongue, had lost its power.

" Well, Ann, what do you think of our
youngest ? " the mistress demanded in her
gayest tone as she stepped into the kitchen.

" I saw you on the lookout as we came by the window."

This was a deliberate tease, and no time was lost in taking up the challenge.

" Me on the lookout, is it? Not fur the likes of him, thin! I seen the two av yez come laughin' up the walk an' the ' Dead March ' playin' behind yez. Sure it 's God's own wurrld fur all the trouble that 's in it, an' there 's plinty to look at besides a giddy b'y like him."

" Well, I 'm not so fond of funerals as you are, Ann. I 'd much rather look at a ' giddy b'y ' who wants to put forty dollars a week into my pocket."

" Forty dollars, is it ? "

" There are two of them — Mr. Embury and Mr. Williams, partners."

" An' where will it all go to? Into thim prospects, like pourin' water down a rat-hole, an' that 's the last ye 'll see av it. Ye 'd better put it in the crack av the flure. It 'll be safe there, anyways." From which will be seen the direction Mrs. Dansken's investments were taking, and what encouragement she found in the bosom of her family.

Before many weeks it became necessary
to add a second story to the main part of the
cabin, and with this Mrs. Dansken declared
she had reached her limit. She had a perfect company, more would be a mob. She
now began in her own way, which was not a
groping way, to materialize her ideal of domestic comfort and prettiness. It became
one of the amusements of her guests to follow her processes. She did not attempt too
much, and so she never failed in the dis-
couraging and pitiable manner of more imaginative decorators. She had no artistic
principles to bother her, she said ; nor did
she pretend to any superior light in a con-
ventional way. She flattered her admiring
constituency by appealing to their own later
standards, presumably higher than her own.
Was it thus, or so, at their mamma's table,
or in her drawing - room ? — not that one
could hope to do more than suggest, but
one's suggestions might as well take the
right direction. She was nothing but an
imitator, but she liked good models when
she could get them.

Mrs. Dansken had a design in these cajol-
eries, perfectly creditable to more than the

business side of her character. Her young men, she was pleased to observe, were getting the habit of rushing home after business hours, to be in time for tea in the much discussed little parlor, which had become the property of all, since each had contributed, by his advice at least, to its development. Many of them would gladly have contributed, out of their absurd young affluence, in more substantial ways, but the landlady was resolute on the subject of gifts. She accepted the help of long arms and strong backs when pictures and curtains were to be hung, and of vociferous tongues on all occasions when her own was not the "dominant persistent," but she preserved her independence of their pockets, beyond the weekly stipend by which she held her own, with something over to put into prospect-holes.

No. 9 was getting a reputation as one of the show cabins of the camp. Nothing was expected of the outside of a Leadville cabin, but there was sharp rivalry as to the comparative merits of interiors. The young men boasted with caution, but it was matter for gossip that Mrs. Fanny Dansken was making her family comfortable in ways that were clever beyond those of the ordinary frontier housekeeper. The practical gifts, after all, are the ones which give a woman vogue among other women. Beauty or personal charm may do more with men, apparently, but women know, and men discover, that these triumphs are slight and temporal compared with the secret, possessed by the few, of an unobtrusive mastery over the means of modern living.

The ladies who were the pioneers of society in Leadville began to recognize Mrs. Dansken's "afternoons" — with the courage of an indifference that was a trifle insolent she had announced herself "at home" on Saturdays — as one of the institutions of the camp; the more readily, perhaps, that Mrs. Dansken's young gentlemen, all of them who could manage it, made a point of getting home early on their landlady's "day," not to miss the exciting privilege of carrying about cups of tea and plates of biscuits, which they subsequently emptied themselves, and chuckling over their performances afterwards with their hostess, in those too brief moments by the parlor fire between dusk and the summons to dinner.

They swore to each other that she was the best little woman in the world — the very woman for the place ; and as they were the very men for the place, there could be no question as to mutual fitness. They knew by heart all the playful, mocking changes of her bright, untender face. It was not a remarkable face, taking it feature by feature, but it kept one interested. Mrs. Dansken had the sort of person, both as to face and figure, which suits the dress of the period, whatever the fashion of it may be ; which is not to say she lacked individuality, but that her individuality had an alertness and a certain hardihood capable of withstanding casual effects of costume. She had exceedingly small hands, pretty in the way which is said to be American, and she used them with charming facility. They were, indeed, prettier to watch than her face ; and the young men used to tell her that a second cup of coffee at breakfast was desirable, for æsthetic reasons.

As a matter of course her name went East, with extravagant praise of her virtues, celebrated in letters to mothers and sisters, who discussed this remarkable woman with a degree of skepticism not unnatural under the circumstances, and wondered if she had charms as well as virtues.

If Mrs. Dansken's experiment was a success, it was because, in the language of the camp, she had put herself into it for all she was worth. The mothers had no cause for anxiety ; it was not their precious sons she wanted, only a little of their sons' precious money. This queen of landladies had no idea of entertaining herself or her boys, as she called them, in a way that would ultimately be bad for business. As for any folly more serious, Mrs. Dansken was a clever woman, thirty-four years old ; marriage for its own sake had no illusions for her, and she would as soon have thought of sacrificing the remains of her complexion to a pink bonnet as of arranging herself for the rest of her life in trying conjunction with a husband obviously her junior. The ages of her boys were charming ages, but they were not the ages that were becoming to her own.

But all this does nothing like justice to her good sense and good faith. She knew that she was in the land of inflated values, where pippins were as good as pineapples so long

as the latter were not obtainable; but she
had no desire to pass for anything other
than the honest, shrewd little pippin she was,
and a last year's pippin at that.   Her young
men, she saw, were of a stamp more likely
to be endangered by the tragic delusions of
the place than by its cheap temptations;
and stoutly she resolved that, if the chance
were given her, she would be as loyal to
them as they had been to her.   In the mean
time she catered for them devotedly.   She
trotted all over the town in search of sur-
prises for those brave appetites.   Every
marketman and purveyor in the place knew
her and liked her, not only for her pleasant,
praising ways, but for her keenness in de-
tecting a substitute for a good bargain, even
when offered with the best of excuses.   The
sweeter side of her nature was coming out
in the sunshine of kind, admiring looks, and
of the chivalrous appreciation she had won
— and all in the way of business.   It was
just the success she had planned, only so
much more gracious.   Her boys had lifted
her life out of its sordidness, and lent a
touch of benignity to her bald little scheme.

When the ladies who were working for the

new hospital came to her for assistance, she told them she was too busy to work and too poor to pay, but she assured them that she was coöperating with them in her own way, by keeping men out of the hospital and out of the places that led to it. It was fortunate for Mrs. Danksen, said the ladies to each other and subsequently to other ladies, that she was able to combine business and charity so conveniently. Her little boast was widely quoted, and came at last to the ears of her boys, much to her chagrin. They did not push the joke too far, seeing that it troubled her; she was indeed far from priding herself upon anything she did for them. They were paying a proud price for more than the best she could give. But there was one service she openly threatened them with if it came in her way. It was part of her duty, she declared, in the station to which she was called, to preserve them — in the absence of their female relatives and of legitimate objects for their affections — from the Western marriage, so often fatal to Eastern boys.

"I may say, *always*," she emphasized. "Eastern women may be wanted in the West, but Western women are never wanted

in the East. Why? Because there are women enough there already — women who are
acclimated, body and soul. And how does it
end? You forsake your East for the sake
of your wife, or your wife for the sake of
your East!"

"There seems to be a good deal of forsak-
ing, whichever way you put it," Hugh Williams, the stout and calm bachelor of the
company, observed in the silence that followed Mrs. Dansken's words.

" Behave yourselves, my dear boys, and go
home and marry your own girls, to the happiness of all concerned. And I shall have
earned the prayers of your anxious parents."

" How do you know but that some of us
may have come out here just on account of
our own girls? Are n't we to have any girls,
East or West?" asked Williams.

" How many of you, I should like to know!
Let the blighted ones hold up their hands."

An emulous brandishing of hands replied
to this demand. Every pair in the room
went up, amidst shouts of laughter — every
pair but one. Frank Embury, with a face
that was scarlet, was stooping and poking the
fire.

"Oh, my poor boy!" thought Mrs. Dansken, seeing that it was her favorite the random shaft had pierced. "You are the one I shall have to look out for."

III.

AT this time, the spring of 1880, there were no girls to speak of, and not more than a dozen married ladies, in the camp. Four of these young matrons were at Mrs. Dansken's on one of her Saturdays, when the young men were at home, making the most of their simple privileges. One of them, a pretty little blonde man named Blashfield (a general favorite, chiefly on account of an artless way he had of exposing himself to general ridicule, and taking it angelically when it came), was trying dance-tunes on the banjo, while the ladies — of New York or Chicago or St. Louis, as the case might be — experimented fitfully with each other's steps in the round dances that were then in fashion. The young men looked on restlessly, protesting that this sort of thing would not do, and the ladies were finally separated, and divided, so far as they would go, among the superfluous sex.

Blashfield's performance was so ungratefully received that he presently put down his banjo and claimed a share in the dancing, to music furnished by his critics. One of the ladies then took off her gloves and played waltzes on Mrs. Dansken's hired piano with verve and passionate precision. The springs of rapture were touched. The merry matrons, blushing like school-girls in the heat of the room, were silently passed from hand to hand, while more and more dancing was the plea.

The late spring twilight, prolonged by snow reflections, stole away and left them circling round by the light of the fire, with a mimic rout of shadows gyrating on the walls above their heads. The ghost of joy was not yet laid when the ladies trooped homewards, with a husband apiece who had come to look them up, and Ann, putting her head in at the dining-room, inquired, "Do yez want any dinner the night?"

This was the origin of a series of dances which called itself, with the touch of laughter inseparable from everything the camp did at this time, the "Assembly." Its meetings were fortnightly, in the dining-room of the new hotel; and here, on Assembly nights, the Cymons and Cœlebs of a crude generation — in flannel shirts, it must be confessed, and "wearing their own hair" — claimed the hands of the lively Jocastas and Pamelas, in dresses they could afford to sacrifice to the new pine floor of the Clarendon. The ladies were amused and flattered to find themselves again on the footing of girls of one season. It was one of the little insanities of the place that these modest and hitherto uncelebrated dames should find themselves temporarily representing the feminine idea. It was a pleasing responsibility while it lasted, and perhaps it was as well that it lasted no longer; for this phase of a new society, when married women frankly do duty for young girls, is one of the briefest.

Before autumn much of the simplicity had departed. The day of competition and of preferences had begun. As the ladies progressed in splendor they were openly congratulated upon their costumes as so much contributed to the glory of the camp, and the first dress-coat made a paragraph in the daily paper. There were other changes, showing how in the newest society the old experiments are repeated in the sequence history has made us familiar with.

The camp was forming into crowds. There were the iron-mine crowd, the famous Chrysolite crowd, the Evening Star crowd; Chicago had its crowd, St. Louis, and New York; and the society of the camp, made up of these coalitions with their respective followings, revived the period of the oligarchy, under conditions, it must be owned, that made the renaissance something of a burlesque.

This picturesque but belated tendency may have been assisted by the presence of the aristocratic element in unusual force. There were many young Southerners, recruited from families impoverished by the war, who brought with them the feudal feeling and the need for personal distinction; there were sons of Northern families, bred in the same exclusiveness, but with more practical adaptability. These young gentlemen, many of them, were incidentally engaged in chopping their own wood, cooking their dinners, and mending their trousers;

but they did these things to their own aston-
ishment and the admiration of their friends,
not in the least identifying themselves with
the part of the laboring-man.

None of the social expedients of the frontier will ever have the fascination of the
"crowd." None of them so completely illus-
trates the boy and girl element so conspicuous in the life of the new West — the mining and engineering and military, not the
rural West. It appeals to those fine romantic instincts, loyalty and personal leadership
in men and faithfulness and concentration
of feeling in women. Woman, who, as the
"Pilgrim's Scrip" says, "will probably be
the last thing civilized by man," is notori-
ously happy in a "crowd," and never more
herself — for to lose herself with a woman
is to find herself.

When an Eastern woman goes West, she
parts at one wrench with family, clan, traditions, clique, cult, and all that has hitherto enabled her to merge her outlines —
the support, the explanation, the excuse,
should she need one, for her personality.
Suddenly she finds herself " cut out," in the
arid light of a new community, where there

are no traditions and no backgrounds. Her angles are all discovered, but none of her affinities. A husband does not help her to be less conspicuous; he is another figure cut out beside her own, often another vantage for attack. She hastens to lose herself in her husband's crowd. She will conform to any restrictions that will secure her in this immunity from general observation, which implies general criticism. And so restful is the sense of support, so emancipating the obscurity, so stimulating the intimacies and passionate partisanships of the inner circle, that it is not wonderful if these privileges are somewhat jealously extended, and only to those who can be relied upon to preserve as well as to enjoy them.

For plainly it is not every one who can belong to a crowd. It is a matter of temperament, of breeding, of religion even, of progress in the lessons of humanity. The element that loves the chatter of the streets and does not mind being chattered about, the honest Samuel Pepys's element, will stay outside; so will the element that uses its friends for ulterior purposes; so will the element that yearns for popularity — the members of a crowd are never popular ; so will most that is broadest, kindest, most human and democratic in our modern life. The crowd is the fortress on the hill, opposed to the noisy, sunny, gossipy streets of the great free city on the plain. It will exist yet for many years on the feudal frontier.

A Western crowd comes easily together on a basis of common interest or convenience, but some deeper sentiment than this is required to give it entity, to make it a force for good or evil. It must have a soul as well as a body. In this respect Mrs. Dansken's house was built upon sand. The only principles on which it rested were personal comfort and the making of money. All beyond was boyish gallantry and extravagance, and the sentiment any woman who is not unnatural can awaken in a generous and pure young heart. So far as moral support went, Mrs. Dansken knew that she had reason to be content ; but she had her little troubles, of a sort the most devoted constituency cannot keep from the door. She had saved out of her experiment considerable money, which she had promptly invested with a courage worthy of better success. Several of her

young men had tried to give her points; but
she did not see her way, she said, out of the
camp that year nor the next, and the young
men were ungenerous enough to say they
were very glad to hear it.

An internal difficulty had also arisen which
threatened the foundations of her scheme.
Without Ann Matthews the business of the
house could not go on; and, whether from
the effect of the harsh mountain climate at
that great altitude, or the pressure of her
work, which was more miscellaneous than she
had been used to, Ann's strength was visibly
on the decline.   Anything like sympathy or
assistance from her mistress she fiercely re-
pelled; but by substituting her own steps for
Ann's whenever on one pretext or another
it was possible to do so, Mrs. Dansken con-
trived to keep the house going, and to shield
her testy old servant from the young men's
criticisms.

"Why do you let her bully you so, and
why do you do *all* her work?" they inquired,
with that air of superior enlightenment as to
methods which no housekeeper can be expected to tolerate.

"She does n't bully me.   Do I look like a

person to be bullied? She is nervous, poor
old thing! It's the climate."

"Does the climate never make you nervous?"

"Ask Ann," said Mrs. Dansken. Ann
would have said that if there were any nerves
in that house they belonged to the mistress.

Mrs. Dansken herself had discovered that
to be the centre of a circle of magnetic young
spirits, whose bodies one has agreed to main-
tain at a persistently high level of comfort
in an essentially uncomfortable place, is not
a restful position for a woman to hold. But
she was determined to hold it, and to hide the
cost. She could not hide the cost from Ann,
who was convinced that her mistress was kill-
ing herself, and so spurred on in the race between the two, which should exert herself and
spare the other more ; but a deliberate word
of affection rarely passed between them.
One Sunday morning when they were making beds together in the extension, Ann was
inveighing as usual against the young men
— the claims they made, and which the mistress allowed, upon her time and strength.

"The more ye do fur thim the more
ye may do! Is n't it enough ye bed 'em

an' boord 'em, but ye must be feedin' 'em
wid the words out av yer mouth an' the
breath out av yer body? Don't I hear ye,
talkin' the flesh off yer bones below there
nights?"

"You think I need my beauty sleep,
Ann?"

"Indeed an' it's little beauty ye'll get
in this place, nor anythin' else, forbye the
money ye'll make wan day an' lose it the
next."

"What we want in this house is somebody young," said Mrs. Dansken, decisively.

Ann looked up from under her brows.
Her head was bent and her mouth distended
with the effort to hold a pillow under her
chin while she parted the folds of the case.

"In the place av ould Ann, is it?" she
presently asked.

"You know very well that I want nobody
in Ann's place but Ann," said the mistress.
"So what is the use of talking foolishness?
You are tired out, and you say that I am.
Perhaps I am. Anyhow I intend to find
somebody to wait upon us both; to give us a
rest. There must be girls in the place by
this time."

" There 's girls iverywhere, if it 's green sticks ye want, or maybe rotten. Ye 'll get no rest, I 'se be bound, out av anythin' ye 'll pick up here."

" Well, there 's no harm in trying," Mrs. Dansken sighed. " We must have more help this winter, with the fires, and the water to carry."

She sighed again that evening, inadvertently, in the midst of the circle lounging about the parlor in various attitudes of repletion, under the depressing effect of the Sunday custom of two meals a day, and both at the wrong time. She laughed, and plucked herself out of her momentary abstraction, as the cause of her sighing was demanded.

" Oh, breakfast too late and dinner too early, and nothing in the house to give you for tea ! ' "

" Come, you were n't sighing about our appetites," said Frank Embury. He looked at Mrs. Dansken with rather a tender expression in his soft eyes. " What is the matter, please ? " he added, lowering his voice.

Mrs. Dansken raised her own, giving him a smile at the same time. " We need somebody young in the house," she repeated.

"Madam, are n't we young enough for you, on an average?" Williams demanded.

"It is a question of my youth, not of yours. I am young enough to be your land-lady, perhaps, but not to be your landlady's servant."

"Ann's servant, you mean."

"Well, Ann's servant, then. I want to hear a young pair of feet — not in boots, if you please — go slip, slip, up the stairs in the morning before I 'm out of bed, not pad, pad, — poor Ann! — and a groan at the top. I positively have to fly to keep her from do-ing things she knows she has no business to, with her lame knee, and the colds she gets."

"Why don't you let her go on, and *be* a martyr if she wants to?"

"Because she would make herself sick, and then *I* should be the martyr, and I don't en-joy it."

"Where is the need of so much work in a house, anyhow?" This unsleeping question was duly propounded, as it always will be in a domestic crisis, by the male members of the family. "All this sweeping, for instance; you only stir up a lot of dust to wipe away when you 've done."

" And who is it fills the water-pitchers, by the way?" asked Embury. "I swear I saw the skirt of Mrs. Dansken's gown whipping round the stairhead when I pulled in my pitcher this morning."

Mrs. Dansken inquired if he were sure that he knew her gowns from Ann's.

" We'll introduce the fag system," said Williams, " and begin with the smallest. Blasshy, you'll please to hop out to-morrow morning when you hear ' Fag!' "

" Fagging is obsolete. We'll go down in a democratic body " —

" In Blasshy's body " —

" You'll stay upstairs, in your beds, where you belong," said Mrs. Dansken. " I don't propose to have a procession of half-dressed young men promenading the house before breakfast. I do my own promenading then, and my crimping-pins are not becoming."

" Fill the pitchers overnight; nothing simpler, I'm sure."

" Extremely simple, you will find, when the water freezes and breaks my two-dollar-and-a-half stone-china pitcher."

" Why do you have pitchers? Have pails.

We had pails," said Williams, out of the experience of the past.

"Pails are squalid," said Mrs. Dansken.

"Frank, were our pails squalid?"

"I should like to know," interrupted Mrs. Dansken, "who the misguided creatures were that mobbed Chinamen out of this camp? Were they men with sisters dear; were they men with mothers and wives?"

"Men with wives they call 'the old woman.' Wives can work cheaper than Chinamen, don't you know, and they don't interfere with the price of men's labor."

"And the rest of you let them have it all their own way, as usual."

"Some of us were n't here; and we did n't come out here to be mayors and city councilmen. And we claim that it is n't a mistake. The Chinese element" —

"Oh, I 've heard all about the Chinese element since before any of you were born! It is a mistake from my little point of view; anyhow, mistake or not, I want you all to keep your eyes open and think of the water-pails — pitchers, I mean — if you see anybody of the female persuasion, who looks young and strong and not too affluent."

IV.

IT was Mrs. Dansken herself who first met with the person answering to these specifications. She was one day at Daniel & Fisher's, the great dry-goods store of the camp, looking at walking-jackets. The salesman had laid one across the padded shoulders of a female torso, clad in pink cambric. "It's an elegant shape," he said, referring to the jacket — "after an English model. Won't you try it on?"

Mrs. Dansken shook her head disparagingly, but kept her eyes upon the jacket, while she meditated whether, after all, it was worth while buying an intermediate garment so close upon winter.

The clerk, misunderstanding her hesitation, opened the door of a back room, where carpets were being made and sewing-machines were clashing through breadths of coarse sheeting, scattering motes through the long beams of light that slanted from the high, uncurtained windows.

"Miss Robinson," he called, "will you step this way a moment?"

"Don't give yourself any more trouble," said Mrs. Dansken; "I shall not take the jacket." But she felt compelled to wait until Miss Robinson made her appearance, brushing threads from the front of her shabby black jersey.

The clerk held out the jacket; the girl slipped her arms into the sleeves without a word, and stood beside the absurd dummy, filling out with a faultless form, the nicely-adjusted curves of the jacket.

"You see, it is perfect," said the clerk, as Miss Robinson slowly rotated on the heels of her boots.

"I see that the young lady's figure is perfect," said Mrs. Dansken. The eyes of the two women coldly met.

"Not more so than yours, I am sure," said the clerk, with a glance at Miss Robinson.

Mrs. Dansken was aware that she herself was responsible for this affability. It was one of the days when she found life intensely objectionable in all its features; and now she included the girl and the jacket and the man who was trying to sell it.

"It would not suit me at all. Thank you," she added, with a curt little bow to

Miss Robinson. The clerk smiled patiently as he refolded the jacket. He amused himself for some time afterwards, standing in the door of the workroom, staring at Miss Robinson, who was rushing a long seam through the jaws of her machine. He made a number of little jokes, at which the other girls looked up and laughed, but the handsome one kept her head down, and blushed with anger.

Mrs. Dansken had put an advertisement in the paper, carefully worded not to attract the wrong class of applicants. Two or three showy young women called, — chiefly out of curiosity, it would seem. She was becoming discouraged when, on the afternoon of the fourth day, she was surprised by a visit, evidently in good faith, from Miss Robinson. The girl looked very nice in her close, plain turban and black clothes. Mrs. Dansken noticed there was a poor suggestion of mourning in her dress. The short afternoon was falling dark, and she had walked fast, as her pure, deep color showed. She glanced about her, rather wistfully, at the pretty parlor in the firelight: Mrs. Dansken liked her the better for seeming not so much at her ease

as she had with the English-modeled jacket
on.

But the girl was tremendously handsome.
Mrs. Dansken told her frankly she should
expect her to give some account of herself,
since, as she said, she had never lived out
before, and could give no references. This
Miss Robinson seemed to have expected.
The two women had a long talk together in
Mrs. Dansken's bedroom, where as the dinner hour approached they took refuge to
escape interruption.

During dinner the mistress was preoccu-
pied with the question, Will she do? It was
her way to make the most of small domestic
incidents for the amusement of the family.
Everything was grist that came to her mill.
It would not have occurred to her to have
disposed of Miss Robinson, even had her
case been less interesting, without first taking lively counsel upon it in the fireside con-
clave. She informed her household that she
had found the "somebody young," and explained, upon being congratulated, that it
must depend upon them whether she should
venture upon her.

"She is n't a servant; she is just one of

the chances of the place; and she is the prettiest girl I ever laid my eyes on, I think."

" Oh, think again, Mrs. Dansken," she was advised.

" You have no idea how pretty she is, unless you have seen her. Have you seen her?" There were conscious faces in the group.

Mrs. Dansken reddened. " Well, if you know my young lady, you must know better than I can if she is possible."

" But who is the young lady, Mrs. Dansken?"

" Don't be evasive."

" Is she the girl with copper-colored hair who runs the machine at Daniel & Fisher's?" Hugh Williams asked, composedly.

" Why, yes, I suppose so," said Mrs. Dansken, vaguely relieved by his manner. " Her hair is rather of the metallic order. What do you know about her?"

" She made me some sample-bags once. She sewed 'em up good and strong, and I was pleased with the way she snubbed a young man who was giving her a good deal of his advice."

"A talent for snubbing will not improve her for my use," said Mrs. Dansken. She perceived from words that followed that there had been some harmless joking about the girl at Williams's expense; the others had perhaps coveted a share in it. She was "out of it" herself, and it did not please her to be "out" of anything that interested her crowd. "It is really very funny that I should set up to introduce you to my discovery. It seems she is your discovery."

"Not one of them ever spoke a word to her, Mrs. Dansken," said Blashfield, in his good-natured, literal way, "except Williams about the bags. She is a very nice young lady. I know she will never look at a fellow on the street."

There was a laugh at Blashfield's modest confession.

"Oh, this will never do," said Mrs. Dansken. "She is n't a young lady. You don't expect to treat her like one, do you, when she comes here to wait upon Ann? How will you treat her, I should like to know?"

"Any way you like," said Williams, who was always obliging.

" No, it 's no use.   You 've begun joking about her " —

" We can leave off, I suppose."

" It 's too bad — and I want her so much! I can see by the creatures that came before her what my chances are if I don't take this one."

" Why don't you take her? I can't see for my life what the matter is."

" The matter is, excess of participation. You are on the *qui vive*, every one of you."

" Because you won't tell us anything about her.   You excite our curiosity and leave us a prey to it. Has n't she a story? "

" Yes, she has a story — quite a pathetic one.   I don't care for their stories as a general thing " —

" Whose stories, Mrs. Dansken? " Frank interrupted, rather impertinently, Mrs. Dansken thought.   She answered with asperity :

" *Their* stories."

" I thought she was n't one of ' them.' "

" She will have to be if she comes here. She does n't come as a *protégée* of mine, or a young lady in distressed circumstances."

" But what is she now? What is her present status, besides running a machine at Daniel & Fisher's ? "

"If you 'll listen you will find out —
that is, if her story is true. Her name, to
begin with, is Milly Robinson. She is a
Canadian — English, not French. That accounts for her complexion, I suppose, and
that indestructible look she has. She had
a brother out here mining. He wrote to her
that he was doing well and sent her money
to come on with. She arrived last April,
with about five dollars in her pocket, and
those red cheeks, which she could n't put in
her pocket. She seems to have expected her
brother would be the first person to meet
her as she stepped out of the stage, and that
his mine would be across the street. The
mine turned out to be a prospect-hole, fifty
miles away, and nobody knew anything
about the brother. She was completely up-
set by this turn of affairs, after her journey
and all. She was sick nearly a month at
the Sisters' Hospital (I wonder if she is a
Catholic). The Sisters were very good to
her. I believe they took her to their house,
and they wrote to the brother's address.
His partner answered, after a while. The
brother was dead, and the partner seems to
have got all the money. His story was that

the brother sold out his share and 'blew it all in' in about a week down at the Basin, and then started for the Gunnison early in the spring while the snows were deep. He started in a condition to miss almost any thing he aimed for, and so he missed the trail, and dropped off, and his horse fell on him " —

"Lively narrative style, Mrs. Dansken has," Hugh Williams observed.

Mrs. Dansken made a little face at him and continued : " After she left the Sisters she went to Daniel & Fisher's ; but she says she cannot stand the machine work. I told her if she was out of health this would not be the place for her, but she said housework was just the change she needed, which is very true ; but I doubt if she is leaving the store on account of her health. She seems to have a certain amount of sense. She is quite willing to take the place on my terms, hard work and good pay, and no question of what she has been used to. I told her she 'd have to sleep with Ann and take her meals in the kitchen. She will be just like the little Irish girl in a cap and apron, who sweeps down your mother's stairs. What I

want to know is, can you treat her the same?
Are you going to make a heroine of her?"

" We will if you insist upon it."

" I 'm perfectly serious. It 's a situation,
I can tell you!"

" A very good one, I hope, for Miss Robinson."

" You may laugh, but it 's not so simple."

" I should think it might be as simple for
us as for her. Do you really want the girl,
Mrs. Dansken?"

" I really do, Mr. Williams; or rather, to
be honest, I don't want her, but I need her."

" You wish to engage the services of a
young person and leave the young person
out of the transaction?"

" Precisely. It does n't sound very amiable, does it?"

" It sounds a little difficult; but if she
agrees, and if it is on her own account " —

" Oh, it is n't. It 's on my account — and
on yours."

" What is the matter with us?"

" Don't you see? I am letting the wolf
into the fold. Here is a girl, beautiful, un-
protected, as they always are, going about
the house as if she were struck dumb; no-

body knows what she is, or what she is thinking about. She is a mystery, while you are
all in evidence. She serves and you accept
her services. Don't you see what a situation it is? Pretty girl-help in a land where
there are no girls."

"Mrs. Dansken, you are a woman of imagination."

"Not at all. However, I believe I have
impressed myself, if I have n't you. I shall
not dare to have her!"

"Oh, you must! For the sake of the situation."

"Never! Unless you will agree to take a
solemn oath — one that will hold water — a
regular iron-clad " —

"Let us have it. We will take it as one
man."

"I shall not give it to you that way. You
are expected to take it solely and separately,
on your individual and sacred honors. I
have my conditions all ready for you. I intend to be explicit. First, you are not to
call Milly ' Miss Robinson.' You are not
to bandy her name about with all manner
of jokes and teasing of one another about
her. You are not to talk to her except in

the way of her work; not to be trying to spare her, or furtively doing her work for her, or wondering if she is happy, or how she stands it, or concerning yourselves about her in any way, shape, or manner. Is that enough?" laughed Mrs. Dansken.

"It is enough to make me feel that I shall probably elope with Miss Robinson — I mean Milly — before she has been in the house a week," said Hugh Williams.

Lightness of touch was not one of Mrs. Dansken's social qualities. When she was gay she was aggressively gay, and when she was morbid she called the household to witness. But even in the enthusiasm of her bargain — she had a pathetic faith in bargains — she perceived that something had gone wrong.

Hugh Williams was fond of this little business woman, and thought it a pity for her, still more for her boys, that she should have given such a blow to her influence in the house. He tried to open for her a way of retreat while yet the lapse of taste might pass for a joke. But Mrs. Dansken refused his assistance. She had meant to be unselfish towards her household, and perhaps she was, so far as her thought went; she felt that injustice had been done both to her judgment and to her motives, and she permitted herself to sulk a little over her mistake. She insisted that she was perfectly serious about the promise she intended to exact from each one of the young men before the anomalous Milly should come into the house. The pledge was giddily and derisively taken by all except Williams, who said it meant something or nothing, and he would have nothing to do with it either way. When he parted with Mrs. Dansken for the night, having outsat the others an hour or more by the fire, he was impelled to venture upon these words: —

"My dear Mrs. Dansken, the charm of this house has been that we are all solid. There has n't been a leak in our mutual confidence. We are solid for you, solid for one another, solid for old Ann. Do you suppose one of us would give the old girl away, — her cooking, supposing it was n't perfect, as it always is, — or permit an outsider to intimate that she had n't the temper of an angel?"

Mrs. Dansken laughed nervously. "And now you want to know if the future Milly

is going to be included in the general
solidity?"

"Yes."

"That depends. She may be solid already, in some other direction."

"Her story does n't sound like it."

"Well, don't you think we have had
enough of Milly Robinson for one evening?"

"I think we have had more than was necessary. I am sorry you are going to have
her."

"I must have her. It's impossible to
keep on in this way, and there 's no genuine
help in the camp — thanks to your anti-
Chinese patriots."

"Can't you import somebody who would n't
be so — conspicuous?"

"She will not be conspicuous, if none of
you make her so."

"But you have already made her so."

"I had my reasons. She is my girl, Mr.
Williams. If you will mind your promises
and let her alone, I can manage her."

"Will she be your girl? Are you going
to make her so, and keep her so, as you do
Ann? You know these boys — they are
bound to see fair play."

" What in the world do you mean ? Do you think I 'm going to trample on the girl ? I intend to treat her as other people treat their girls."

" How do people treat their girls in a place like this, where, as you say yourself, there are no girls ? We both see the situation, but you see it only as it affects us. Consider one moment : would n't it be safer — for us — if you should look at it from the point of view of the young woman ? "

" What do you wish me to do — have her in the parlor evenings to entertain the company ? I think you are insane on the subject of Milly Robinson. However, it 's not for you that I concern myself."

v.

THE first evening of Milly Robinson's ordeal, when she appeared, blushing high above the soup-tureen, Mrs. Dansken thought the unconsciousness of her boarders somewhat overdone. It was not likely, however, that the girl would perceive it. Her excessive color was the only sign of embarrassment she showed. She had a very good manner. Her long, silent step and precision of movement were restful, and showed that she was not going to be overcome by her new position. After all, was she so alarmingly pretty? Crimson cheeks and copper-colored hair, even with streaks of gold in it, did not go particularly well together. Large hands implied large feet. On the whole, Mrs. Dansken was rather ashamed of her oaths and conjurations. She had had no reason, however, to suppose that the young men were taking their vows much to heart. They were strolling about the parlor after dinner, lighting their cigars, as they were privileged to do; Embury was stooping to poke the fire, laughing, with his face to the room, when Mrs. Dansken saw his expression change.

Milly had put aside the portière, and stood, with the coffee-tray on her hand, looking about her for a table. There was something admirable in her controlled hesitation, in the presence of a roomful of strangers who had all turned to look at her, unprepared for her appearance in place of the familiar figure of old Ann. Her eyes sought those of her mistress, who silently directed her towards a low table, where she placed the tray. She then retreated, getting herself very nicely out of the room with one more look at her mistress, as if to ask if all were right.

The parlor lamps had not been lighted. The fire-light reddened her figure as she stood a moment, facing the room, in her black dress and wide, white apron, against the dull blues and greens and orange of the curtain. Amber lights floated in her full eyes under the soft shadow arched above them; all the color in the room, revealed in the dusky fire-glow, seemed to focus in her hair.

The latest arrival among Mrs. Dansken's guests was a young man, unaccounted for except by the name of Strode. Williams had not been thinking of Mr. Strode when he described the house as solid. Strode was tacitly held as an outsider, partly because he belonged distinctly to one of the crowds in the camp with which Mrs. Dansken's crowd had no affiliation.

As the curtain fell behind Milly this young man showed his teeth in a smile of appreciation, and noiselessly clapped his applause. Not another smile was to be seen in the

room.   Mrs. Dansken preceived this as she
did many things, sometimes when it was too
late.

"They are solid for Milly," she reflected,
and she resented this championship of a
stranger, on the part of her crowd, before
the crowd's mistress had signified her consent.

"Did you ever see anything more perfect?" she exclaimed. "The room was all
cluttered up with you, every one of you staring at her, and she did n't see a single soul.
And did you see her look at me?" She ex-
patiated upon the girl's manner, which she
explained was that of a perfect servant,
provoking an argument as to whether the
qualities which go to make this vaunted
manner in the servant are not much the same
as those which distinguish the perfect mistress, since to each belong self-control, tact,
and carefulness for the wants of others, com-
bined with an absence of fussiness. Mrs.
Dansken was quite sure this was a subject
heretofore of little interest to her young
men ; and the side she took in the discussion
did not gain in popularity by the fact that
Strode was her only ally.

Embury was at the piano, trying the accompaniment to a tune he was whistling, when Milly came back for the coffee-tray. " Go on ! " Mrs. Dansken was obliged to whisper. The young man did not look particularly grateful for the hint.

" These are the preliminaries ; we shall get used to our minion after a while," she said, as Milly left the room.

" How easily ladies call names ! " Embury murmured, smiling.

" I suppose because when we were little girls we did n't get kicked for it, as little boys do," said Mrs. Dansken, with her usual frankness.

When the young men went to their rooms that night, each found his candle lighted, the fire intelligently laid, window-shades drawn down, pillow-shams — one of the hostess's troublesome little household fopperies — neatly folded out of the way. Each occupant surveyed his arrangements with complacency, if with some amusement, at this latest step in the direction of their landlady's ideal for which the new maid must be responsible. Each man emptied his precious water-jug and set it outside of his door.

Smiles were exchanged across the passage.

"I shall leave my slippers in the wood-box to-morrow morning, just to see what becomes of 'em," said Blashfield to his next-door neighbor.

"Old Ann would heave 'em on the dust-heap."

"But Milly won't, you bet!"

"Blasshy, we'll report you," said another voice.

"What for?"

"Taking the name of Milly in vain."

"Look here, boys; I shall have to tie a knot in my watch-chain if I've got to remember to" —

"'I have struggled to forget,'" the voice sang out, "'but the struggle was in vain!'"

The young men came down to breakfast next morning, each, with the exception of Williams, wearing a bit of blue ribbon in his button-hole. Somebody, it was evident from the raveled edges, had sacrificed a neck-tie. Mrs. Dansken dared not ask the significance of this decoration; but when Milly was gone it transpired that they were Mrs. Dansken's good little boys, and had taken an oath which the blue ribbon would doubtless

help to remind them of, since it was such a
very slippery oath — Blashfield having already foresworn himself the very first night.

Mrs. Dansken confiscated the ribbons before the young men left the house, and made
them into a breast-knot which she wore in
her dress at dinner, to the intense delight of
the boys, who forgave her the oath`for the
sake of the fun they intended to get out
of it.

Ann, as a matter of course, was bitterly
jealous; the more so that she could find no
reasonable ground for objecting to the new
favorite. She called her "The Duchess,"
and scouted the idea that she had never
lived out before.

"Look at her hands!" said Ann.

"Well, look at mine! Look at everybody's hands in this place, with this water
— and, suppose she has lived out, what difference does that make?"

A very great difference it made to Ann,
whose experienced services were thrown
quite in the shade by those of the alleged
amateur. Her undisputed honors as cook
failed to console her for the suspicion that,

as a waitress, she had not been considered a success.

Mrs. Dansken was relieved to find that Milly took little notice of Ann's hostility. There was a cool self-sufficiency about the girl, or an apathy, which gave her an attitude of singular independence in the midst of the life of the house, from which on all sides she was excluded. Her fellow-servant had not made common cause with her; her mistress, she had understood from the beginning, was to be merely the other party to a bargain, by which, as Hugh Williams had put it, the services of a young woman were to be secured and the young woman left out of the question. Mrs. Dansken admired Milly's philosophy. " I should behave just so in her place," she assured herself; but she found herself thinking about the girl much more than she had intended, more indeed than was restful. Practically Milly had been left out, but she was there all the same. Her mistress fancied there was something uncanny about the girl, some hint of experience beyond her years, which sustained her in the blank isolation of her life. For she had no outside support; her connection with the camp had ceased, apparently, from the day she became one of the family at No. 9. But then Mrs. Dansken bethought herself how easily an older woman can make mistakes about a young girl; how apt she is to exaggerate meanings or the absence of meanings, to think her stolid or secret when she is merely shy.

Nothing, meanwhile, could have been less sinister than the aspect of the household sphinx. She bloomed like a winter sunrise. The work which two women had found oppressive, divided among three went smoothly on, and Milly's share seemed no more than the exercise her vigorous youth required. She went about the house, with her look of intense life, seen of all but looking at no one, hearing all the household talk but never speaking, ministering to comforts in which she had no share. It is appalling to think how starved her importunate young egoism must have been; how few words were said to this young girl, during her first months of service, which had any personal value or reference to herself; how many were lightly tossed over her head, between the gay, privileged young men and the mistress, who was the providence of the house.

Did all this difference lie in the fact that one was employed and the others were employers?

The oath was kept with ironical ostentation. It was Mrs. Dansken who could never let the name of Milly rest. She eulogized the girl continually, but always in her menial capacity. Perhaps she insisted too much, for one evening when Milly's name was introduced, as usual in connection with her exquisite usefulness, Williams said in his moderate way that one might suppose, from the remarks that were made about her, that Milly Robinson had come into the world labeled " Mrs. Dansken's Second Girl."

" Now when Frank and I were baching it," he continued, " I used to cook the grub, but I did n't give myself out as a cook — not generally. I continued to retain a small portion of my individuality; enough to keep Frank up to his work, which was the dishwashing, you know."

" That is a perfectly childish argument. If you had come here and cooked my food, I should have given you out as my cook, and treated you accordingly, and not very bad treatment either: ask Ann."

" Illustration is n't argument, of course : I only wished to ask you if you think we are to be classed strictly according to our occupations," said Williams.

"It depends upon the occupation. The occupation of a servant makes a servant, for the time being, unless the occupation is neglected ; in that case the servant is a bad servant, and had better try some other occupation."

" Then if I should elope with Milly, — as I 've been thinking of doing, you know, just as soon as you can find another girl, — and we should come back after a while, and ask you to make room for Mrs. Williams at the table, then the other girl would be the servant, and Mrs. Williams " —

" ' Illustration is not argument,' Mr. Williams, and there is n't going to be any argument or any illustration, I hope. I captured the position to begin with because I knew just how it would be with you theorists. Wait till you get servants of your own and wives of your own to manage them. I think the wives will agree with me."

" Well, we have n't got to the wives yet. It 's an abstract question with us so far."

"It's never an abstract question. It's always a question of a particular person when you come to live in the same house with them. In this case it's a question of a very pretty girl."

"It is just possible that even a pretty girl may be human," said Frank Embury.

"We're sure to hear from Frank when the pretty girl needs a champion," said Mrs. Dansken. "And what is there about Milly's position here — which is altogether voluntary, remember — that strikes you as inhuman?"

"I think I know one or two pretty girls who would n't care to change places with her."

"We cannot change places in this world, my dear boy. We have our little fitnesses and unfitnesses, and we'll find ourselves in the long run pretty much where we belong."

"I should hardly say it had come to the long run yet with Milly Robinson. How long is it since her fitness for this place was discovered; and what was the place she fitted before she came here?"

"Well, when I saw her first," laughed Mrs. Dansken, "she fitted a very nicely made walking-jacket they were trying to sell me at Daniel & Fisher's."

"What, Mrs. Dansken?"

"She was trying on jackets for customers at Daniel & Fisher's," said Mrs. Dansken, explicitly. "How would your pretty girl like that?" No one answered; and Mrs. Dansken, in a very good humor, asked them then if they had ever heard the story of the princess and the wishing-chair. "Ann used to tell it when I was a little girl. Could you listen to a story, supposing I can remember half of it, and make up the other half?

"Well, once there was a king who had six beautiful daughters; and in one room of the palace stood the wishing-chair on a dais, with a curtain before it, and on her sixteenth birthday each of the princesses in turn was allowed to sit in the wishing-chair and wish the wish of a lifetime. The youngest princess was a madcap. She made fun of the stupid old chair and of her sisters' wishes for jewels and castles and handsome young husbands, that would have come of themselves in due time. She said when her turn came she would wish a wish that would show what the old chair could do.

"There was a prince in that county of Ireland very wealthy and powerful, and he was bewitched, so that he was obliged to spend half of his time roaming the country in the shape of a terrible wild roan bull, and he was called the Roan Bull of Orange. Now the youngest princess, when she got into the chair at last, turned rather pale, and she wished, while her father and mother and all the happy sisters wept and pleaded, that she might be the bride of the Roan Bull of Orange. And then she flew out of the chair and hugged them all round, and said that it was all nonsense — the chair was as deaf as a post, and the Roan Bull would never hear of her wish.

"However, he came that night, trampling and bellowing about the house, and demanded the princess. And the princess went and hid behind her mother's bed. They took the daughter of the hen-wife instead, and dressed her up in the princess's clothes and packed her off; and when the Bull had carried her on his back across the hills and the valleys to his castle, he gave her an ivory wand and charged her, on her life, to tell him what she would do with it; and she sobbed out she

would shoo her mother's hens to roost with it.
So the Roan Bull took her on his back again,
and over the mountains with her, and
slammed her down at the door of the king's
palace, 'fit to break every bone in her body,'
and demanded his princess. After they had
heard the hen-wife's daughter's story they
took the daughter of the swineherd, and
charged her, if the Roan Bull gave her an
ivory wand, she was to say she would guide
her milk-white steeds with it; and so should
she save the life of her dear little princess.
But she thought as much of her own life, it
seems, as she did of the princess's, or perhaps
she was so frightened she could n't speak
anything but the truth; for when the Roan
Bull gave her the wand and glared at her
with his awful eyes, she said nothing at all
about milk-white steeds, but whispered she
would drive her father's pigs with it. So
back she went like the first one, and was
slammed down at the door, and this time the
Bull fairly raved for his princess. They had
an awful night of it in the palace, for the
princess had 'got her mad up,' and said she
would have no more of these silly substitutes.
She took the Bull by the horns, as it were,

and off she went, in the clothes she had on ;
and when the wand was given to her she said
without the least hesitation that it would be
very convenient to beat the maid with who
did her hair, when she pulled the tangles in
it.   So the Roan Bull knew he had got the
right one at last; and if you don't see the
application " —

"But what became of the naughty little
princess?"

"Oh, miracles were performed to save her
from getting what she deserved — I don't
remember that part ; it never seemed real to
me, like the other.   What I wish you to observe, is the Roan Bull's ingenious way of
testing for metals.   And there my illustration comes in, don't you see; for when dire
necessity gets us in a tight place, and puts
the wand of opportunity into our hands, we
discover pretty suddenly that we are what
we are, neither more nor less, and some of
us turn out to be keepers of highly select
boarding-houses, and some of us wait on the
boarding-house table, and we do it much better than if we had been born princesses."

" And I hope you respect yourselves more
than if you had gone and hid behind the bed,

and let some one else face dire necessity in your place."

" Of course we do. I don't say we are not much better than princesses, only we are different. We could n't change places without being found out. Now I insist that Milly Robinson, who seems to be the text of all our sermons lately, has somehow got the sort of discipline that makes it possible for her to live in this house in the way you see. It 's very strong, if you like, and very admirable, but I don't feel called upon to be a bit more sorry for her than I am for myself."

" I don't see why you should n't be sorry for yourself, if you want to. You were not born a Leadville landlady, were you, Mrs. Dansken ? "

Mrs. Dansken blushed. " I don't know what I was born. I know that I am one *pro tem.*, and not so very *tem.* either. As you say, it 's better than hiding behind the mother's bed, but I really do not feel there is any great virtue in it, so long as there is no mother's bed to hide behind. My point is simply this : your mothers could not be successful where I have been successful, thanks to you, my dear boys, and yet not *all* thanks to you. Your sisters, probably, would not suit me as well as Milly does, in Milly's place. But I hope you don't think it's anything against them. I don't; I could n't imagine one of your sisters trying on jackets at Daniel & Fisher's."

The young men considered this second reference to the jacket unfair; Mrs. Dansken herself knew that it was, since exhibiting jackets on her person had not been Milly's occupation. She forgave them, therefore, the heat of their reply. But the retorts on both sides were now too hotly engaged for mutual consideration, much less strict justice to the cause of the fray.

"How do I know what she was, or is, for that matter? I have only her word for it. They make a great point of never having lived out, when the most of them have never been so comfortable, nor so cared for, in their lives before."

"'Them' — 'they!' Who are 'they,' Mrs. Dansken?"

"Anybody who is n't us," said Mrs. Dansken.

A silence fell upon the room as the shutting of a drawer was heard, and the door leading from the dining-room into the kitchen closed quietly.

The combatants looked at each other rather sheepishly.

"You are safe, my dear boys. She could only have heard the voice of her natural enemy."

The voice of the "enemy" had the quality which carries.

PART II.

THE SITUATION DEVELOPED.

I.

It was two months or more after Milly came that Mrs. Dansken began to fancy the situation was becoming strained. The weather was now extremely cold; the ice on the water-cask of a morning was so thick that it was necessary to cut it with a hatchet. In doing this Milly had cut her hand, and again there was an uprising on the subject of the water-pitchers. Mrs. Dansken was immovable and logical, as usual.

Had it ever occurred to the young men to inquire how the little woman who did their washing managed to get her tubs filled, this winter weather, with the "ditch" half a mile from her cabin? It had not occurred to Mrs. Dansken to make active inquiries on this subject herself. She considered it was none of her business; nor was it the

business of her young men to concern themselves how their water-pitchers were filled.
Both were paying to have these things done
without inquiries. But for the sake of con-
sistency, would they tell her how they could
put on a clean shirt without thinking of the
woman who washed it — a little woman, not
half so big as Milly, and an old woman at
that? " As for the little scratch Milly has
given herself — well, it is n't the fashion to
speak of such things, but you should see
Mrs. Murphy's wrists! If you can only
accept service that costs nothing, you 'll certainly have to wash your own shirts."

After breakfast Strode handed to Mrs.
Dansken an unopened pot of vaseline.

" What 's this for ? " she asked.

" For the wrists it is not the fashion to
mention."

" Oh, I gave her some myself. Even a
hard-hearted person like me can spare a little vaseline. Pray keep it, or give it to
Milly. If we should take up a contribution
for her wounds, she might anoint herself
from head to foot, like a Fijian bride."

This time, decidedly, there was temper
shown on both sides. But the little washer-

woman told Mrs. Dansken, with tears of gratitude, when she came with her weekly basket, how kind the young men had been — how they had sent a man to dig a little channel from the main hydraulic mining ditch to her cabin, so that now she had the water at her door.

Mrs. Dansken knew that this tapping of a main ditch meant considerable trouble as well as money, but she did not attempt to sully the widow's gratitude by casting doubts upon the motives of her benefactors. It was Mrs. Dansken's opinion that one motive was as good as another, so long as the result was the same.

As Christmas drew near, the subject of gifts was mooted. The young men made sarcastic allusions to the rules of the house, and asked if their oath permitted them to remember the waitress, as well as the cook. "As a waitress, certainly," they were informed. And how were they to make it sufficiently understood that the remembrance applied to the waitress to the exclusion of the girl?

"Easily enough," Mrs. Dansken explained, with gravity equal to their own. Let the remembrance take the form of a general gift from them all to Milly, not from each one of them to Miss Robinson.

It might be difficult, the young men objected, to unite on a single gift that should represent them all.

Would they find it difficult to unite on a gift for Ann?

The session broke up with something of the old hilarity ; only Mrs. Dansken insisted that the gift should be appropriate. The term was allowed, without discussion of its application to a gift for Milly. But an opportunity was not long delayed for further elucidation of Mrs. Dansken's views on this subject.

A few of her guests, among them Frank Embury, were in the habit of knocking occasionally at the door of the sitting-room where she betook herself to wrestle with her accounts, or make over her dresses, or hold consultations with Ann. She had drawn closer in these days to the older woman, and liked a quiet talk with her on matters which had been their own before the stranger had come into the house.

Frank knocked and entered with a pile of

books under his arm; they slid to the floor as he took a seat. Mrs. Dansken was careful not to look at them too closely, thinking they were for herself. Frank saw that she thought so, and this made it more difficult for him to say that they were for Milly.

Mrs. Dansken recovered herself, and looked at the books with the most amiable interest. "Is this the general gift?" she asked, wondering not a little at the choice of a modern edition of Miss Austen's novels.

"No," said Frank. "It is something I thought of doing on my own account; or, rather, of getting you to help me to do."

"You wish me to help you give these books to Milly Robinson?"

"Yes — that is, they are submitted first, of course, to the public censor of gifts."

Mrs. Dansken did not like to be called names, though she could sometimes give them to others with great facility.

"Frank!" she exclaimed, "really it seems almost perverse of you to insist upon this sort of thing! These are books you could give your sister. Why do you wish to give her books?"

"I don't wish to give her poor ones.

That 's the kind she seems to be reading now."

" Dear me! How do you know what she reads ? "

" Oh, I happen to know," said Frank.

" But these are books entirely over the head of a girl like Milly. Have you ever read Miss Austen ? "

Frank owned that he had not.

" I have n't either, but I 've got an idea she is a sort of fad nowadays, like old miniatures and paintings on velvet."

" Oh, I don't think she 's a fad. My sisters were reading her in an old edition that belonged to one of my aunts — board covers and paper labels and jolly rough edges."

" Well, your sisters may come naturally by their Miss Austen in board covers. I don't mean she would be a fad for everybody. 'Pride and Prejudice!' 'Sense and Sensibility!' Now, Frank, do you suppose when Milly Robinson has got through one of these books — which I doubt if she ever does — she will have the faintest idea what even the title means ? "

" I don't know, I am sure," said Frank, sulkily. He was not so confident himself about his choice, which was one reason for indulging ill-humor now that it was being criticised.

" Oh, well, give her the books if you want to," said Mrs. Dansken, relenting in amusement at his disgust. " She will be the chief sufferer."

" I wanted you to give them to her."

" Well, I shall not! She 'd think I was making fun of her."

" Then keep them, and read them yourself," said Frank, maliciously.

" No, you must take this admirable female back, and get something of Mrs. Whitney's — no, Mrs. Whitney writes about high-toned servant girls. I 'm afraid she would be demoralizing. Are n't Grace Aguilar's books read a good deal by young girls? "

" By young servant girls, do you mean? "

" I 'm afraid we would not make much of a committee on books for girls, Frank," said Mrs. Dansken, forgiving him entirely now that she had made him lose his temper. " Don't you know any books that are safe and easy to understand ? "

" That is the kind I read," said Frank. " I 'm afraid the ' Weekly Light of Home ' is n't very safe."

"Is that what Milly reads?"

"I think so, sometimes."

"Well, I must look after her reading, for your sake. But I wish you would tell me how you came to know so much more about it than I do?"

"It 's not much that I know. You could easily get the inside track of me there."

Mrs. Dansken seemed struck by this expression. "The inside track! Yes, of course, there are two ways of getting there. Don't you suppose I know that my way is n't the true way? Frank," she exclaimed in a burst of harassed confidence, "if I could only be fond of the girl, as I am of crabbed old Ann — if I could make her like me and trust me, as Ann does! Well, I should know all about her then — more than any of you could know. But I cannot do it. Good people, I think, have no likes or dislikes." (Mrs. Dansken always spoke of good people with toleration as a race by themselves, alien in some sense to the rest of humanity.) "I would like to make Milly believe that I like her, but she has her intuitions. I would get rid of her, if I could possibly get on without her. I hate to acknowledge what a difference she has made in the house. And yet, there are days — oh, well, this is all ' nerves,' don't you know? Did you ever find yourself nursing an antagonism? You have no idea how it occupies the mind. It 's as exciting as the first stages of a love affair."

"How queer women are about their business relations," said Frank. "They are so personal. Men never think whether they like each other or not. They get on together all the same."

"So do I get on. Don't I get on most beautifully? I 've never had a word with Milly — and yet there are mornings when I wake up and think, I 've got to go down stairs and say, ' Good-morning, Milly ! ' and look at her without meeting her eyes. She never looks at me ! — Well, I wish I had the house clear of her and the work just as hard as it was before."

"Mrs. Dansken, you are certainly morbid."

"I told you I was. I 've let myself go. Do you see anything uncanny about her, Frank? Honestly, apart from all our badgerings, does she seem to you a nice girl?"

"I don't know anything about her, Mrs. Dansken, or about girls anyway. You know they are all mysteries to us."

"'They,' 'us'!" said Mrs. Dansken, in great irritation. "I'm not asking you about Milly Robinson as a *parti*."

"Do you mean, do I think she would steal the spoons?" shouted Frank.

"There are things in this house besides spoons that do not belong to a girl in Milly's position."

"Good heavens, Mrs. Dansken! Have we any of us any position that we can hold all alone? Are we blocks of stone in a quarry, set up alongside of one another?"

"Frank, I wish you had a block of stone in place of that soft heart of yours."

Frank blushed angrily. "Yes, when people talk about other people's soft hearts, they generally mean their soft heads."

Mrs. Dansken laughed outright at this; and before Frank carried the estimable Miss Austen away, the quarrel was made up.

"Superintend her education, if you want to," were Mrs. Dansken's parting words. "I shall not interfere. I won't have it on my conscience that if I'm not good myself I keep others from being good."

In spite of the little taunt, Frank understood that Mrs. Dansken meant to trust him in all that concerned Milly. He was too young a philosophizer about women to be able to conclude how much of her confession was a true mental record and how much had been evolved in the excitement of controversy and self-revelation. His own simple judgment in the matter was, that if she would stop thinking that she felt thus and so about Milly, she would cease to feel so.

For several days after Mrs. Dansken's talk with Frank, in which she had let her aversion see the light of day, she felt its hold relax. She refrained from watchfulness; she did not refer to Milly as the Sphinx, or the Phenomenon, or the Perfect Treasure : she spoke of her by name, quite simply and humanly, without any exhibitory adjectives. She looked her antagonism in the face and saw only a pretty girl in an attitude of set, despondent passivity, and of continuous hard work. She could not accuse herself of having failed in her part of the agreement under which Milly had been glad to come; nor had Milly, on her own part, ever complained or protested.

Why, then, should Mrs. Dansken have dreaded to meet the girl on the stairs, or alone in her bedroom, engaged in those intimate services we call menial, which are assuredly as difficult to accept as to render in a forced relation?

II.

On Christmas morning, after a late breakfast, the tree was lighted in the darkened parlor, and the family gathered around it. Ann and Milly came in after the others had assembled, and stood a little apart, but not together.

Two of the young men gathered the fruits of the tree and gave them into Mrs. Dansken's lap as she sat in the most prominent place in the room and called the names attached to the gifts. She had not meant to watch the effect of the young men's "remembrance" upon Milly; but when the cumbersome box was handed to her, containing a muff and cape of long dark fur, which Mrs. Dansken had selected, thinking of the color of Milly's hair, curiosity as to how the girl would demean herself overcame her. The manner of accepting a gift is one of the tests of breeding, even more than the manner of giving, since the passive part is always the hardest.

"From the young gentlemen, Milly," said Mrs. Dansken. "Won't you open it?" she added, as the girl took the box and held it awkwardly, looking discomposed rather than happy.

Milly sat down — there was no chair very near — and bungled with the string. One or two of the young men looked at her, but most of them found something to take their attention elsewhere. Ann regarded Milly's part with toleration, holding her own present on her arm — a fur-lined mantle, of a quality of silk superior to that of her mistress's, as the latter had playfully remarked, adding that she should have to borrow Ann's cloak when she wished to be fine.

"Do cut this string, somebody," Mrs. Dansken demanded on behalf of Milly. She looked at Frank Embury, who immediately looked away. The string was cut and the cape unfolded from its paper wrappings.

"Now let us put it on you, Milly," she

said. " We must show them how it becomes
you. I feel responsible, because I chose it."
She was helping Milly to disburden herself
of her gratitude, if it were that which oppressed her. More likely, in Mrs. Dansken's
opinion, the girl was sulking because she
had thought Ann's present handsomer than
her own.

Milly submitted to be dressed in her
costly gift before the eyes of the givers.
There had been nothing from Milly to the
young gentlemen. As a matter of course
the liberty to give belonged to them. Her
part was to accept and be thankful. She
stood up, looking embarrassed and sullen,
and said, without raising her eyes, that she
was very much obliged to the gentlemen.
And then suddenly she looked at Frank
Embury. His eyes met hers with an inex-
plicable expression of humility, of apology:
Milly may have understood what the look
meant.

Mrs. Dansken saw it, but in her mood of
forbearance she would not permit herself to
take alarm.

There was a dance that evening in the
parlor of No. 9. Ann, who had exhausted

her energies on the Christmas dinner, had
been dismissed to bed. At ten o'clock a
waiter from the Clarendon knocked at the
kitchen door with a parcel of cakes and a
form of ices. The mistress, on the alert in
the midst of the lanciers, signaled to Embury.

"Go and help Milly," she whispered.
"Show her how to dump the cream."

Frank took this command as a recognition
of the new compact between them, as well as
a concession to the spirit of the day. But he
gave her an arch look of inquiry, as if to ask,
"Do you really mean it?" Appealing glances
from other partnerless youths, propping the
walls of Mrs. Dansken's parlor, signified their
desire to be of use, but were laughingly par-
ried.

As the dance went on, subdued sounds of
voices and steps and the quiet tinkle of silver
could be heard behind the dining-room curtain. An occasional bumping of plates be-
trayed to the housekeeper's ear the unpracticed masculine touch. Mrs. Dansken was
tired of her vigils. "What business is it of
mine?" she asked herself. "Let nature
have its way." But nature's ways are wild

ways, under conditions that are not legitimate — when the wives usurp the young
girls' places in the dance, and the young girl
of the house has no friends in it, and no par-
tisans, except the young men of the house.
Mrs. Dansken had created this situation, had
set it on wheels, confident that she could
steer it safely and make profit to herself out
of it.   But the vigilance of suspicion is never
so sure or so . untiring as the vigilance of
love.   Mrs. Dansken's way was the way of
all expedients, by which we hope to avoid
the consequences of some fundamental ill-
adjustment in our plans.

At eleven o'clock, when the supper was
over, the mistress said : " You may go to bed
now, Milly ; I shall not call you till half-past
seven to-morrow."

No mistress, not the most forbearing, could
have liked to be smiled at in the way in
which Milly smiled whenever Mrs. Dansken
tried to be, as she called it, " nice " to the
girl.   At such times Milly herself was not
nice, nor pleasant to look at, for all her
prettiness.   The impression blotted all the
back pages of Mrs. Dansken's mental record
of the girl ; she seemed to have been always

smiling in that unpleasant way, without raising her eyes.

Milly locked the silver-drawer, put the key
in its place, and returned to the kitchen.
Here she remembered that she had not her
kindlings for the morning fires, and taking
an old shawl from its nail behind the door,
she wrapped her head and shoulders in it
and went out.

The night was clear and piercingly cold.
Her breath made a little cloud before her in
the moonlight as she crossed the trodden
space between the kitchen and the wood-
shed. At the door of the shed she encoun-
tered Mr. Embury with his hands full of
light-wood and shavings sifting dust over his
evening trousers.

"I heard you say that you had forgotten
your kindlings; and it's so late, you know,
and so horribly cold" —

Certainly the thing he was doing, waiting
upon Mrs. Dansken's waitress, called for an
apology, even to the waitress herself.

He was bareheaded. The wind was blow-
ing up the short locks from his forehead. He
looked very kind and handsome, but, as he
felt, very much out of place.

Milly held out her apron. "Run in; run in, quick!" he commanded. "You'll freeze to death!"

She laughed excitedly as she ran before him into the kitchen and closed the door upon them both. It occurred to Frank that he had never heard her laugh before — he had never heard, in the camp, a girl's laugh that was innocent.

Milly drew out from behind the stove a box into which Frank noiselessly deposited the kindlings. The kitchen lamp, not smoking, as kitchen lamps are apt to, but burning clean and clear, showed the state of his trousers.

"Shall I slip up stairs and get your clothes-brush?"

"No," he said, beating himself with his hands.

"Let me sweep you off, then. I've a clean broom in the closet here."

He stood up, laughing, to be swept down. "How about this?" he said, glancing at the spillings of his handful of kindlings on the floor. "Ann will know you never did that." Instinctively, and without being at the least pains, he was as secret as if he had spent his life in kitchen conspiracies.

" I 'll sweep it all up," said Milly. " I 'm
sure I 'm much obliged," she added ; and although she looked at him as if she expected
him to say good-night, Frank noticed that she
seemed happy and at ease.

" It 's late for you to be up. You must be
very tired," he said, raising one foot to the
stove hearth and leaning his arm on his knee,
in an attitude for conversation.

Milly softly lifted one of the covers of
the stove and stirred the coals into a glow.
The kitchen, with its lamp turned low, and
its one cold, moonlit window at the dark
end, took on a look of extreme comfort and
seclusion.

" 'Most always I 'd rather sit up than go
to bed," said Milly, reflectively.

" Don't you get awfully sleepy with no
one to talk to evenings ? "

" Yes, no one but Ann ; I suppose it 's
because she is almost always sick, but she 's
awful cross. She wants the whole bed. I
wish she had it. I 'd a good deal sooner
sleep on the floor, if it was n't so cold."

Frank did not know what to say to this ;
there was an appalling frankness about it
as a revelation of the undercurrent of life

in the house. A sudden irruption of male
voices and footsteps from the parlor into the
dining-room brought him to a sense of his
own position. Milly looked at him in undisguised alarm. She made haste silently
to cover the light of the stove ; and as she
blew out the lamp and slipped into the pan-
try, a young man, hitherto unpracticed in
hasty retreats into back regions of his
friends' dwellings, found himself cooling his
hot face in the moonlight among Mrs. Dansken's wash-tubs and water-barrels, reflecting .
upon the fact that of all the men in the
house he had got himself chosen as the
worthiest of its mistress's confidence.

For several days after the episode of the
kindlingwood, Frank's behavior to Milly
took on a tone of extreme loftiness. He
had scarcely spoken six words to the girl
before that evening, except such as Mrs.
Dansken might have indorsed from her own
point of view ; yet the change in his manner
was felt by Milly as distinctly as if he had
tapped her on the head by way of enforcing
it. She resented the young man's accession
of dignity and copied it faithfully, so far as
the negations of their intercourse permitted

the one who served to copy the manner of the one who was served.

From his attitude of dignified reserve Frank lapsed suddenly into an extreme fit of homesickness. Visions of his cousin, of the marshes and the shore, swept in upon him in a great wave of bitterness that obliterated the tide-marks left by the restless risings and fallings of his spirit. He was honestly sure of his case; so sure and so unhappy, and so lonely in his unhappiness, that one day when he took his landlady out on the Soda-springs road for a sleigh-ride, and they had plunged along for a mile or more in silence, he was moved to unburden himself. It was a natural but most unfortunate incident of his friendship with Mrs. Dansken, confirming her, as he did, in his present faith and perfect openness, his sorrow and preoccupation, and convincing her later of his duplicity.

There is no untruthfulness so confounding as that which a perfectly sincere nature occasionally can perpetrate. Frank came home from this ride intrenched in Mrs. Dansken's confidence, and in his own belief in the incurableness of his old love. In his

pity for himself he was very tender, very
lenient, to the sufferer. He felt he was en-
titled to all that woman's friendship can do
for one whom love for a woman had blighted.
And if he was tender with himself, he did
not forget to be tender towards others. He
felt very old and beneficent when he thought
of Milly. He decided that he would forget
all about that ridiculous scene in the kitchen,
and, above all, cease to visit his annoyance
with himself upon her. Had he been more
than simply helpful, as a man should be to
women, in all circumstances? Would he not
do the same thing again if it came in his
way? — with this difference: he would not
retreat among the wash-tubs, and leave poor
Milly to think he was ashamed to be seen in
her company. If his breeding could not
support such a situation as that, what was
breeding good for?

Mrs. Dansken held out her hand to him
when they parted after their ride, at the foot
of the hall stairs. Because it was a pretty
hand, and because its owner had been kind
to him in ways he could never return, he
stooped and kissed it. As they stood in this
attitude, as becoming to a tall young man

with a charming profile as to a little woman with a pretty white hand, the dining-room door opened and Milly Robinson appeared, with a freshly ironed tablecloth upon her arm.

"Excuse me," she said, avoiding Mrs. Dansken's stare of inquiry.

"Well, what is it?"

"The wash is n't home yet, Mrs. Dansken, and this is the last tablecloth in the drawer, and it 's got a slit in the middle."

"Put one of the table-scarfs over it — the one with the poppies."

"I thought you did n't want them used every day," said Milly, stung by the insinuation that the interruption had been needless.

"It is n't every day we have a slit in the tablecloth," the mistress retorted, sharply.

Frank was shaking with laughter as he went along the hall to his room; but between the two women there was no merriment.

III.

THERE was another dance at No. 9, this time an impromptu one, an evening or two later. Ann and Milly, who were not on duty, were supposed to be in bed and asleep. Ann was asleep, but Milly, restless with the sound of the music, had crept up the staircase, past the door of the parlor, where all went merry as a marriage-bell, and seated herself on one of the upper steps, with her head against the partition wall, listening with benumbed attention to the soft tread of feet keeping time to the continuous beat of the music.

She roused as the piano stopped: there was a discussion of some sort among the dancers, and Embury, who was obliging and quick on his feet, shot out of the parlor-door and up the stairs in quest of Blashfield's banjo.

In his charge upon the staircase he had very nearly tumbled over Milly before he perceived her, crouched on the steps in shadow. He passed her, as she rose, with a look of surprise and a hasty apology, fumbled about in Blashfield's bedroom, seized the banjo, and found himself face to face with Milly again, in the dusk upper hall.

"I did n't mean to go bowling into you like that," he said. "I did n't know you were there."

"I was listening to the music," Milly explained, looking at him earnestly, as if to compel his attention.

"Are you fond of dancing?" Frank asked, kindly.

Milly did not answer; she hesitated as if she had something more to say. Frank smiled at her encouragingly.

"You won't speak of it in there, will you?"

"Speak of what, Milly?"

"You won't say I was sitting on the stairs? She 'd ask what was I doing there, before them all; she 'd think I was listening."

"Milly, you ought to know there is no one in this house thinks such things of you as that."

"She does," said Milly. "She thought I was listening that time in the dining-room. You were all talking so loud — I could n't

help it. I heard her say she was my enemy,
and so she is! I would n't stay here if I had
any place to go to."

" Child, you have n't an enemy in this
house. Mrs. Dansken was only joking.
Don't you know her way? I must have a
little talk with you some time, but not now
— I must go back now," said Frank, distracted at the possibility of a relief sent out
from the parlor for the recovery of himself
and the banjo, and forgetting his resolve to
face whatever contingency might arise in his
championship of Milly.

" Is anybody keeping you? " asked Milly,
bridling.

" Yes, you are keeping me — you poor —
sweet " — The banjo softly boomed against
the banister. Milly released herself, and
Frank was left alone at the stairhead, with
the astonishing consciousness upon him that
he had just kissed Milly Robinson. He was
never able to explain to himself how he came
to do so; but the fact remained, and also
the fact that he must return to the parlor
with that kiss added to the other suppressed
entries in his account with Mrs. Dansken.
And besides his account with Mrs. Dan-

sken, there was his account with Milly. How is a young man to make a girl, who is relegated socially to a sphere below his own, believe that a kiss, given in secret and accompanied by words of endearment, is merely a token of respectful sympathy?

For several days he thought about Milly continually, seeking opportunities to speak with her, and shirking them when they came. Her conscious looks alarmed him. He had a foreboding that he should get himself into further trouble if he recurred to that meeting on the stairs; yet to let it pass without a word seemed like assuming that Milly was accustomed to being treated in that way and expected no apology.

His cheeks burned when he thought of Mrs. Dansken's probable comments on such a situation; and when he thought of his cousin, the girl he used to know so well, but who was now estranged from him in ways she could never dream of, he knew it was not the decrees of parents that had put that distance between them. He was restless and miserable. The attraction of his thoughts to Milly increased in proportion as he blamed himself for his conduct towards her. The idea that he had wronged her, and that he owed her some reparation, came to have a charm for him. He dwelt upon it, and at last came the inevitable talk with Milly.

There was more than one talk perhaps before Frank found himself in a position which made it necessary for him to bring his case again before Mrs. Dansken. The submission of Miss Austen was a trifle to this, he knew; and his heart was thumping as he knocked at the door of the little sanctum where judgment awaited him. He took a long breath, and went in.

It was about a week before the evening of the next Assembly Ball. Mrs. Dansken was preparing a dress for the occasion, out of material furnished by one that she had laid aside some years before as " too young." Her Leadville season had been so reassuring that she had been led, urged by economical reasons as well, to reconsider certain resolutions as to colors and styles. The woman who hesitates on a point so delicate as this is usually the better for a little unprejudiced advice from some near member of her own family. There was no such person to come to Mrs. Dansken's assistance ; the dim, side

light upon her mirror was delusive; she was
actually embarked upon the venture of a
Nile-green silk, and was ripping the breadths
of the train when Frank came with his
troubles to her door.

She blushed a little over her finery as she
admitted him, but he was much too self-ab-
sorbed to have known whether she were making a ball-dress or a shroud. She wondered
what the young man could have upon his
mind now. Could he have had bad news
from home? — had the family relented, as
she had freely assured him they were certain
to do? He did not look particularly happy.

"Are you very busy?" he began, frown-
ing absently at the gay disorder about him.
"There's a little thing I wish to speak to
you about."

It is not a little thing, Mrs. Dansken concluded, as she looked at him; but she smiled
encouragingly, and deposited her lapful of
silks upon the sofa.

His eyes followed her anxiously about the
room. "It's the forbidden topic, Mrs. Dansken; but you said you would trust me —
about Milly, you know — and of course that
puts me on my honor."

Frank found it difficult to say these words. Some of us may know the impulse of self-mortification that impelled him to urge them upon himself, and he had his intentions to support him.

"It's not her education this time; it's her amusements. She hasn't any, you know," he added, as Mrs. Dansken did not speak.

"Hasn't she?" said Mrs. Dansken, curtly. "I'm very sorry, but I did not promise to amuse my waitress when I engaged her."

"You did not promise to amuse your boarders, but you have done much more for us than feed and shelter us."

Mrs. Dansken flushed. No woman likes to be reminded by a man that she has been kinder to him perhaps than was necessary.

"Then be modest about your privileges," she said, "and don't be trying to instruct me in my duty to others."

"I had no such idea, Mrs. Dansken; I ask only your permission — I want to give Milly a good time, myself. Just one good time, such as any other girl might have."

Mrs. Dansken sighed. "How do you propose to give it to her — from your superior station above her? In that case I don't think she will enjoy herself."

"Of course not. I don't mean to be superior. It's going to be partly my good time."

"It's going to be, is it? Then why do you come to me?"

"You know why, Mrs. Dansken."

"But you have already smashed our contract all to pieces."

"You absolved us from that first contract. You said I should do as I pleased," said Frank.

"It seems you *have* done as you pleased. Now if you will tell me *what* you have done" —

"You make it very difficult. If I tell you why I wish to do this, you will say I am instructing you."

"You need not tell me all the whys. I want to know what you have been about."

"I have asked Milly to go with me to the Assembly, Friday night."

"Then all I have to say is, you have made a precious fool of yourself!" But this was not all she had to say, by any means; for directly she added more gently, feeling that she had lost ground at the outset in losing her temper, "Frank, it is simple madness."

"But listen to me, Mrs. Dansken. Here is a young girl who goes nowhere" —

"She has every Wednesday afternoon to go where she pleases," Mrs. Dansken interjected.

"But the fact is, she goes nowhere. Where could she go, in a place like this, with no friends?"

"Is it my fault that she has been here nearly a year and has n't a friend in the place?"

"It may not be her fault either."

"It 's not my fault and it 's not my business; still less yours, Frank Embury! I don't say I have done my perfect duty by Milly; I 'm not perfect in any capacity; but as to your duty, there is n't the slightest question. From this moment you are to leave that girl alone!"

Frank looked the anger he felt. Mrs. Dansken could not know what had led to his inviting Milly to the ball; her unmitigated view of it only made him feel prouder

and more apart from all such poor, low con-
structions.   But, for Milly's sake, he must
temporize.   He knew he could not afford to
dispense with the countenance of an older
woman for the girl he sought to distinguish.
So he shut down upon his wrath and pleaded
with all the ingenuity he was master of, and
with all the power of his charming looks —
never more needed nor in a more unhappy
cause.

"Let us talk it over in the abstract, for
the sake of the humanities " —

"For the sake of the fiddlesticks! I don't
wish to hear any more of this missionary
talk. You know perfectly well that if Milly
Robinson was not a stunning-looking girl
you would n't be seen with her at the Assembly. But don't you see, Frank, — of
course you see, — that only makes it the
worse for her ? "

Mrs. Dansken too was condescending to
plead, from the force of her alarm for Embury. It was the soft-hearted, headstrong
boy she feared for, not the girl, with her
curious, passive force, that drew to her
everything that she wanted, without an effort of her own. She had not the least

anxiety for Milly; but she knew that she could only reach Milly's champion through the girl he was crazily befriending.

"It is one of the things that cannot be done, Frank," she patiently explained; "because when it is done it cannot be undone. Nothing can ever be as it was before, between you and Milly, after you have had one dance together. And what is to come next? How do you propose to get back into real life after this masquerade?"

Some access of excitement altered the expression of Embury's face. His brilliant eyes looked away from the cogent common sense of Mrs. Dansken's argument. She was not sure that she had touched the right string, but she kept on, striking more or less at random. "And how do you propose to ask her? If you ask her as a young lady, she must have a chaperone; if you ask her as my servant, she must come to me for permission to go, and I shall certainly refuse."

"But tell me why, Mrs. Dansken. Is it truly for Milly's sake, or is it that theory of yours that we are all in danger of spoiling our little futures?"

"There are plenty of reasons before we

come to your future. There are the rules of the Assembly, after you have demoralized all my rules. Every gentleman is allowed to ask two ladies — not two persons the other members may not care to meet."

Frank made a movement of impatience.

"Don't listen to my words; listen to my meaning. I can't stop to choose my words. Now *I*'d just as soon dance with Milly, or with Ann either, as to wipe dishes or make beds with them; but I've no business to make it awkward for the others. You'll find the St. Louis ladies are particular whom they dance with. I'm hardly up to the mark myself. The woman who works for her living must expect to rank below the woman who has got a husband to work for her."

"Why do you say those things? You know they are not true."

"They are perfectly true. I haven't enough prestige to make Milly go down with the others, if I were to try. I might take her to the Assembly under my wing and say, 'Here is a nice little girl who does my chamber work. I've brought her to have a good time, because she has nowhere else to go.' Do you think they would help her to enjoy herself ? She would be the stray chicken in the hen-yard; they 'd peck her all to pieces. And there is sense in it too. You can easily see, if each one of you is allowed to use his private judgment as to what constitutes a lady, in the sense of a partner, why there are other young persons in the place — you must see I 'm not narrow about this. It is simply one of the things all the world knows is impossible. Milly is all right as she is; she is n't having a very good time, but it is only six months since her brother died " —

"Ten months," Frank corrected.

"And she is saving money to go to her friends, and they are the ones to look after her. She will have plenty of time to amuse herself after she is done with this place. But take her and set her up in a position that antagonizes everybody — why, she 'll be attacked right and left. This is what would happen if I undertook to set her up; but if you should try it, Frank Embury, she will be lost. And whatever comes of it you will have to see her through."

"I intend to see her through. I have asked her as I would ask any girl, and I shall

not insult her by backing out, on account of
the sneers of the women. There's no sense,
nor justice, nor kindness in it."

"Justice and kindness you'll find are lux-
uries, my child. Minding one's own affairs
is the main business of life — and paying
one's debts, and keeping one's promises."

Embury was hard hit this time, but he
was past wincing.

"Just to show you, Frank, how these
things work : I'm not in the least angry
with you, who really deserve it, but I have
lost every bit of faith I ever had in that
girl."

"For Heaven's sake, what has she done?"

"Nothing, perhaps ; but I feel it is her
fault, all the same. It's the fatal twist in
the situation. You'll find it will meet you
at every turn."

"Suppose she refuses to go. How will
the situation strike you then?"

"Has she refused?"

"She hasn't accepted."

"Oh, she means to go. If she didn't,
she would have told you. It was really very
clever of her to reserve her answer."

"I don't know why you call it clever. I

thought it rather a pitiful acknowledgment that she was not her own mistress."

" Is that what she said ? "

" She said nothing."

" Ah, she has a talent for saying nothing. She is a very deep young person. Her friends, if she has any, are not anxious about her, I think; she has not received a letter since she came."

" Do you bring that up against her ? "

" I 'll bring up anything against her I can possibly think of, to keep you out of this mess you are getting yourself into. It will all come upon *her* in the end. If you had picked out the right girl, — any girl who was possible, — we should all be only too glad to give her our blessing. We should be enchanted with a real young girl, an *ingénue*, in the camp at last. But she must be the genuine thing. We are not going to be imposed upon. Women are always the judges of women, and men who have any sense accept their judgment. They scold and they sneer at us, but they expect us to keep society in order, while they do as they please outside."

Mrs. Dansken's philosophy was often unpleasant to Frank, but in his present temper it was revolting.

"This may be true, Mrs. Dansken, but I don't see how it applies to Milly Robinson. Is there anything in her appearance that would not do for an *ingénue?*"

"Her appearance is the whole trouble."

"Or her story?"

"Oh, her story! What do I know — it 's *her* story. I traced it as far as " —

"Mrs. Dansken, I swear I cannot stand this!"

"Of course you can't. You are young Romance, with a touch of modern philanthropy, and I am middle-aged Common Sense, without any philanthropy at all; but it 's Milly who is going to be the victim."

Mrs. Dansken did not believe that Milly would be the victim, but she thought it well to say so. "But what nonsense this is! To put it plainly, one of my boarders has been meddling with one of my servants."

It was the fate of this facile talker often to say the word too much, and to make it the word that stings.

"You have been very kind to me, Mrs. Dansken," Frank began, in a tone of lofty forbearance.

" I 've been very fond of you, but you need n't spare me on that account. Be as furious with me as you like, but let that girl alone. Promise me you will, Frank. You can't think how serious I am. I have a hard way of putting things, I know, but I am frightened for you both. It is n't possible you can be so innocent as not to see what I mean."

" Mrs. Dansken, I suppose you know we fellows all have our record here in the camp. We are pretty well known for what we are. Well, I 'm not ashamed of my record. If I take a girl to a dance where there are ladies it will be because she is a nice girl, and she will be none the worse, in the eyes of the men at least, for any little attention I may show her."

" Oh, my dear, it 's too pathetic to hear you talk ! You are a lamb — a pair of lambs if you will — going to the sacrifice. It 's perfectly idiotic, but it is the pitifulest thing I ever heard of. And I have got to stand by and see it done ! Look here, Frank," she continued, with a change of tone, seeing that he was unmoved. " You say Milly has not told you yet if she means to go. If she does go, if she accepts, I shall know how to place her. *She* has no illusions, you may be sure, as to how she will be received. If she goes to that ball with you, she deserves whatever she may get."

In the upper hall, after dinner, Mrs. Dansken found Frank standing by the frosty window, a figure of expectation or of despondency, she wondered which.

" Will you listen to one word more ? " she ventured.

" As many as you like," said Frank, so civilly that she knew his impatience had cooled into resentment.

" If you will let me, I will speak to Milly ; kindly, gently as I know how. I will tell her you have spoken to me about her going, and that I have discouraged it for her own sake."

Frank smiled his disbelief in Mrs. Dansken's influence with Milly — the girl for whom she had confessed she entertained an aversion.

Mrs. Dansken felt the smile and the implication keenly. " That will let you out," she continued — but now she had lost faith in this her last appeal; " and if I can't make her see what a mistake it would be for her, it will be because she does not wish to see. If she is the nice girl we hope she is, wild horses could not drag her there ; and if she is n't, — if she is a brazen, pushing thing, — surely, Frank, you cannot wish to take her ! If you had the record of an angel you could n't carry it through."

Frank was himself anxious as to what he was doing, and how it was going to end. He would not for pride's sake have had Mrs. Dansken know how, purely by accident, as it seemed, and without the least intending it, he had got so far on this path of perilous kindness. If a happier word could have been spoken it might have helped him in this moment of indecision. But the slip could not be recalled — the allusion to his boasted record, the intimation that he desired his release, and the epithets awaiting Milly's decision.

Is there any better thing that breeding can do for us than to develop our sympathies, so surely and on such fine lines of divine instinct, that we cannot make mistakes in these delicate dealings with those whom we are brought into relations with ? The habit of thinking kindly, the quality of gentleness and precision in speech, are trifles perhaps, but trifles are occasionally decisive — since it is not enough to be in the right, and to have stern common sense on our side, when it comes to influencing passionate and stubborn young hearts in moments of precipitation.

Frank hardened his heart, and Mrs. Dansken hardened her own ; and as she hardened she lapsed into coarseness as well.

" I believe you are bent upon nothing but your own selfish pleasure and your triumph over the other men."

Frank turned and went into his room and shut the door in her face. He did not appear at dinner, nor in the parlor until late that evening, and then he came in looking cold and pale, but refusing a seat by the fire and taking a book so far from the light that he could not possibly have been able to read it.

Mrs. Dansken had been mentally prefiguring a scene there was little likelihood of her having a chance to enact, or of wishing to do so should the chance present itself. But here was the opportunity, and here was

the audience, without which a dramatic pre-
sentation would fail of its effect. Her im-
aginary climax suddenly took possession of
her, with all the force of a calculated decision. There sat the foolish fellow she had
flattered with her confidence, who had given
her his in return, who had made her believe,
unbeliever as she was, in the sincerity of his
pure, young grief. She knew the force of
her arguments better than the quality of her
words ; nothing, she believed, could have
withstood them but a deliberate courting of
consequences.

She spoke up in her ringing voice and in
a strain of high sarcasm, informing upon
the culprit who had stolen a march upon
them all and made good his intentions before
declaring them. But as her voice began to
shake she abandoned sarcasm for a plain
statement of the case, in a silence that gave
to her words the force of a tribal judgment.

"You know we agreed, about Milly Robinson, that if any of you fellows found he
could n't keep faith with me, he was to let
me know ; and if he broke his word in-
nocently, and it came to be found out, he
was to have warning." As Mrs. Dansken

recapitulated the terms of that famous agreement, it sounded very silly and unreal, like child's play — like vulgar child's play; but there was no amusement in the faces set towards her own.

She was white with despair at the thing she was doing. "And if he persisted, after he was warned," she went on, "we said, you know, that he was to be 'fired out.'" She laughed weakly, but the laugh was all her own. In the silence of these grave faces it had the effect of a sob. "But what shall be done," she went on, "with one who was released from all his promises because I was ashamed to let him promise anything, I trusted him so? He said himself he was upon his honor; and he asks me now if he may take my waitress to the Assembly and if I will introduce her."

"No, Mrs. Dansken; I never asked you that. The girl I take to the Assembly shall need no introduction more than you do yourself. And you may consider my room vacant, if you please, after to-morrow."

"Is this to punish me?" she asked, rather wildly — "a pecuniary punishment, for a mercenary woman who was once your friend, Mr. Embury."

Frank was at the door. He looked at her in utter amazement, made her a bow, and left the room.

IV.

MILLY had said nothing to her mistress, and Mrs. Dansken was still in doubt as to the girl's intentions, when Frank, the next morning, was moving out of the house.

The late friends did not refuse to "speak." That would have been too childish; and there were practical topics on which silence would have been inconvenient, not to say ridiculous, as it would have called for the intervention of a third party; but they were brief and sadly cold with each other.

Mrs. Dansken hung about on various pretexts while the packing was going on, feeling that she had been extreme, and hoping the boy would relent. Middle age is often hard, but it is not so hard as youth, when it comes to a collision.

Frank was taking down his pipe-rack from the space it had decorated on the parlor wall, and the pipes were hanging at all sorts of critical angles, while his eyes sought a place to rest the rack upon.

Mrs. Dansken suffered a little heart-break at the sight of each bare space where one of his "things" had been. He was a young fellow possessed of many "things," not always kept in the most perfect order, which borrowed very quickly a suggestion of his own personality. Mrs. Dansken could tell his belongings without looking at them, his books and odd gloves and silk mufflers, when she picked them up about the house. His hats were a portrait of him, his old slippers would have been a sort of fetish to one who held him dear. In his sweetly imperious way he had required a good deal of waiting upon; he would be missed when he left the house, Mrs. Dansken knew, but not for the trouble he had made. More and more she felt how lovable, how human, he was, how helplessly drawn towards humanness in others; and as the time for his departure came and she marked his excitement, that was not all triumph, she was more sure than ever that some occult reason lay at the bottom of his lunacy.

There was never an emptier place than Frank's at dinner that evening. The household to a man were on the side of the offender. Mrs. Dansken felt that she was in disgrace at the head of her own table. It was so like men, as she said to herself — or, rather, it was so like boys ; and unhappy as she was, she found some comfort in the characteristic unfairness of the situation.

But she did not greatly care ; her dream of leadership had vanished. She wished for her sensible old ally, Hugh Williams, that she might take counsel with him, and be scolded by him, as usual. He had gone, three days before, to one of the new camps to examine a mine, and would not be back until Friday. She sat down that evening and wrote him a long letter, setting her anxieties before him. A reply would be impossible, but she trusted he might get her news in time to hurry home and use his influence with his friend.

Frank had begun to realize for what stakes he was playing, with the pretty partner whom fate and his own rashness had set before him. The silly counters had been removed, and in their place were risks he could not pretend to ignore. But the excitement of the game had gone to his head.

He was obliged to take his departure without seeing Milly, owing, he believed, to Mrs. Dansken's diplomacy; but it was the girl herself who had quietly defeated his efforts to speak to her and to get her answer. He knew her list of outside errands, and the time of her comings and goings. On Monday and Thursday evenings she went to the Tent Bakery to fetch a certain kind of breakfast-roll promulgated on those days. The bakery was at the extreme end of Harrison Avenue, on the same side as Mrs. Dansken's, close to the new bridge that was then being built across the hydraulic ditch. It was not half-past five o'clock, but the workmen had left the bridge; Frank did not know for what reason, but he mentally noted the deserted look of the place.

At the hour which had been the gayest and happiest in the landlady's parlor Frank took his station on the bridge and watched for Milly. He had not long to wait before he saw her coming. She had a brown veil bound tightly over her hat; he would have liked to see her face, and her beautiful pure color in the winter cold, yet the veil was well. He caught the rich burnish of her low-knotted hair as she whisked into the bakery. The bakery was crowded; it was a long time before she came out. In a moment he was at her side. She seemed not much surprised to see him. He took her warm parcel from her, and asked her, in a tone of command, to go back with him to the bridge. He marched off with the bundle of rolls and she followed him.

"How late is it?" she inquired as they reached the bridge.

"It is n't half-past five," said Frank without consulting his watch.

"Won't you look, please?"

"It is n't necessary. I want only five minutes, Milly, for your answer. You are going with me Friday night?"

"No, I never said I 'd go."

"But you mean to go?"

"I could n't go, any way at all. You ought to know that, Mr. Embury."

"And is this all you have to say to me, Milly?"

Apparently it was, for Milly was silent. Frank felt that he would like to take her by her pretty shoulders and shake her, just to wake her up, now that matters had come to a crisis. "Milly — oh, do take off that veil! How can a man talk to a brown veil?"

Milly's lips closed on a little fold of the veil, and then expanded. She did not wish to smile, but she could not help it. These new, peremptory ways of his were even more fascinating to her trampled vanity than his humilities and explanations had been.

"I know your cheeks are the color of that light on the mountains," he went on with wild irrelevancy. "Oh, if you would look at me, Milly!" This was undisguised love-making, Frank knew well; and making love, even to a brown veil, and with a bundle of rolls warming the inside of his arm, came easy to his temperament. (There could be no question as to the angle of his nose, which M. Coquelin considers decisive in this rôle.) The boyish reckless side of his nature had now got the upper hand of him; he considered that he had paid the price of his escapade, and he would not now be balked of whatever excitement there might be in it.

"Come over the bridge a little way, Milly. See, here is the plank."

"I 've got to get home, Mr. Embury; and I could n't go to the ball, not if you were to keep me here all night."

"Oh, stop that eternal Mr. Embury! Why did n't you tell me so before?"

Milly did not answer. "You said nothing. I thought of course you meant to go. You have cheated me, Milly."

"You are so quick — I can't ever talk to you."

"I am quick because you are so slow. But I like your slowness; it 's sweet, if you 'll only give me what you make me wait for. I consider that you have as good as promised; I shall hold you to it."

"Not if it lost me my place?"

"You will not lose your place. Mrs. Dansken told me herself that she could n't get on without you." Frank gave this information unhesitatingly, regardless of the way in which he had gained it.

"She never told *me* that much," said Milly. "She would n't give me the satisfaction. I 'd like to go, if it was only to show her I 'm not the dirt under her feet."

"Oh, no, not for that; but to dance with me. You need not mind Mrs. Dansken, or any of the women."

"I can't go, and I never meant to go, Mr. Embury, whatever you may think. I've got my reasons."

Frank hesitated, thinking of the brother with whose memory Milly might be shyly keeping faith, through all his obtrusive blandishments. He felt rebuked and drew away from her, out of respect for the modest grief he had been wounding.

"Couldn't you tell me what the trouble is? I didn't mean to tease you, but I did want you to have this one good time."

"It's my clothes," said Milly, reluctantly. "I've got nothing I'd look fit to be seen in."

Frank laughed. His respectful mental distance from Milly instantly decreased, and he said gayly, "Oh, we'll fix that all right, if that's all."

"But Mrs. Dansken's got all my wages for two months back, and I won't go to her — not for a penny!"

"Of course not. I will send you a dress, Milly. I can't send you a bouquet, because there are no flowers to be had; but you shall have the prettiest dress in Leadville, and it won't cost more than the flowers a girl carries sometimes to a party in New York. I speak of it so you won't mind taking it."

"I could n't take it from you, Mr. Embury. She 'd know I never bought it."

" Milly, you are in the cruelest position that ever a girl was in in this world, and I intend to set you right, to put you where you belong. Who are they, I should like to know, setting up to tell us whom we shall dance with! A man dances with the girl he chooses, as a general thing. I have chosen you, dress or no dress. But we will see about the dress. I shall be here Thursday, at the same time. I shall expect you. Now run home with your parcel!"

Frank had got to the point of believing that the Old World and all its traditions were wrong, since otherwise he, in his present undertaking, could not be right. He even persuaded himself that it was a romantic and touching thing that he should be clothing his partner out of his own pocket for the dance. He went about his purchase with shy ardor, wishing that he had studied the details of a girl's evening costume more thoroughly ; for he was resolved that nothing should be wanting to complete Milly's triumph, and his own.

PART III.

THE CATASTROPHE.

I.

AT ten o'clock on Thursday morning Mrs. Dansken answered a knock at her front door and found there a man, whom she recognized as one of the waiters from the Clarendon, who presented her with a box addressed to Miss M. Robinson. It was a large, flat, white box such as tailors and dressmakers send home their wares in. There were no wrappings or bills of expressage on it; evidently it had not traveled far. Mrs. Dansken asked the man if there was no message with the box. He said he did not know of any, and Mrs. Dansken refrained from the question who had sent him.

Now if Milly Robinson had been like any other girl, Mrs. Dansken meditated, she would have been in a flutter over that box; would have wondered who had sent it and what was in it, and have opened it at once, for all to admire. Instead, she had packed it off, without any excitement at all, to her bedroom in the attic, and no more had been heard of it.

Ann had made tea-cake and there was no need for Milly to go for rolls that afternoon. At her usual time of coming down, after changing her dress, to lay out the tea-things in the parlor and set the table for dinner, she did not appear. Instead of calling her from the stairs, Mrs. Dansken took the trouble to go up to her room. The girl did not open to her knock at once; she held the door ajar, a very little way, to answer her mistress's demand when she would be down.

"I'm coming, right away, ma'am." Mrs. Dansken fancied the voice from within the room had not quite a natural sound. An excuse for entering occurred to her simultaneously with the resolve that she would get on the inside of that guarded door.

"Let me come in, Milly. I want to measure the sash of your window. Ann says one of the panes is cracked."

"Ann told her that two months ago," Milly said to herself. "I'll give you the size of it, ma'am," she said aloud.

" You have n't time; it 's five o'clock now. Let me come in, Milly."

Mrs. Dansken's voice was peremptory, but again there was a pause before the door was yielded. Milly had her dress on, but the waist was still unbuttoned, though she had been in her room, Mrs. Dansken knew, three quarters of an hour. The quick eye of the mistress, roving the room, perceived that the covers of the bed had been turned back, but that the pillows were smooth.

" Were you going to lie down, Milly? Don't you feel well ? " As she spoke, insincerely, for she believed that Milly was perfectly well, she saw protruding from the bedcovers a white sleeve, an evening sleeve, shortened to the elbow and delicately finished with lace. So, then, there was something beneath, which the covers had been hastily thrown back to hide. With one of her quick movements she flung them into place again, exposing the guilty box upon the bed, its contents crammed into it, hurriedly and unsuccessfully, as the white sleeve bore witness.

" What is this, I should like to know ? " Mrs. Dansken demanded in a high, exasperating voice. Forgetting her own intrusion on a false pretense, she gave way to the thrill of anger and disgust which possessed her. She felt that she could almost have struck the girl for her stupid, coarse concealments. "What have you got here that you are ashamed to show me?" She tilted off the box-lid with the tips of her fingers and looked contemptuously at the pile of soft wool and lace and ribbon that represented Frank's first essay in the part of King Cophetua.

"That's a very handsome dress to be tumbled about like that. Were you going to put it on to wait on table in?"

Milly had been silent because her shame and rage had simply taken away her power to speak.

Mrs. Dansken herself was trembling from head to foot; she was losing control of herself, and felt that she could not be accountable for what she might say next if that girl continued to stand there, smiling faintly, in a fixed way, and as speechless as a stone.

"I will see you by and by. You and I must have a little talk." She went down to her room and threw herself upon the bed; all the strength had gone out of her.

"Ann," she whispered, when the old woman came in to ask her what had become of Milly, "that girl will kill me yet!" But there was no time to get comfort from Ann. Dinner was served, and the hostess must be in her place at the head of the table. "Ann, go upstairs, will you, and tell Milly to come down." The farce must go on, and mistress and maid must take their parts. Mrs. Dansken sickened at her own, but she was eminently a woman of business.

There was a long pause after the soup, which Ann herself had brought in and removed. "Where is Milly?" Mrs. Dansken asked, as Ann reappeared with the chicken patties.

"She 's packin' her things!" said Ann.

Mrs. Dansken whirled round in her chair. "You will ask her to please come down and attend to her work at once. She can pack her things to-morrow."

"Mem?" said Ann.

"Excuse me," — Mrs. Dansken put down her napkin and looked at the tableful of boarders : her voice was unsteady, — "Ann will wait upon you," she managed to say. Blashfield sprung and opened the door for her, and every man at the table rose as she left the room.

She had meant to get to her own room as quickly as possible for an outburst of tears, but she felt so upheld by this unexpected return of the old loyalty that she was ready to encounter even Milly. She was sure that she could be calm, perhaps she could be just to the girl; for what had she discovered, after all, that was so heinous, considering the way she had discovered it? Sympathy, delicacy, dignity, Mrs. Dansken had not; but honesty, even with herself, lay at the bottom of her soul. She ran up the cold attic stairs in a better mood for a talk with Milly than she could have hoped for; but Milly was not there. Her trunk stood in the middle of the room; her hat and shawl, and the box from off the bed, were gone.

II.

MRS. DANSKEN had lain long in the darkness of her own room. Faint sounds from the dining-room told that dinner was quietly progressing. "If they had just

carried me out a corpse they would go back
to their chicken patties," she reflected, and
laughed feebly to herself, not in the least
resenting this conspicuous masculine trait.
"It would be a tribute to the patties, anyhow," she added in her musings. The darkness was peaceful, and she was glad, after
all, that she had not been able to see Milly.
"She must have gone out into the street for
a moment to get some one to come for her
trunk. She will want her wages, and it is
better she should go without any more words
between us. We were never meant to live
together. We bring out all that is worst in
each other. Even Ann sees that."

At this moment Ann came stumbling in
with a clinking tray, which she placed upon
a chair by the bed while she lighted the
lamp.

"Are ye sick?" she asked, turning to
look at her mistress.

Mrs. Dansken could have kissed her grim
old face, for the sense of nearness and confidence it gave her. After all, was there
any one in the world she cared for more
than for this old bit of wreck saved from
the home that had gone to pieces so long

ago? She fell to weeping weakly on her pillow, while Ann felt of her hands, and pulled up the down quilt over her shoulders.

"Oh, I 'm roasted!" said Mrs. Dansken, throwing it off. Then she nestled down again, murmuring, "Thank you, you dear old thing; I knew you would n't forget about me."

"Ye better take a drink o' this tea. Are ye worryin' about Milly Robi'son? Sure it 's better she 's goin'. I knew ye 'd never do with the likes av her. She 's nayther one thing nor another. I 've not got a ha'porth agin her, myself. I c'u'd do with her well enough. Where 's yer shawl?" Ann looked about and found it, and attempted to put it about her mistress's shoulders as she raised herself in bed. "Are ye layin' here widout any fire?"

"I don't want any fire. This tea tastes so good. Ugh! I 'm as hot as fire and as cold as ice! I 've had such a scene with that girl, Ann. I hate a row except with you."

"'Deed an' ye 're not much afraid o' me, that 's a fact. Was it along o' the frock she had sent her?"

Mrs. Dansken nodded.

"She 's not so much to blame for that, as I can find out. 'What 's in it?' says I, whin I see the box layin' on the bed. An' whin she opened it she went red in the face, an' says she, 'I know who sent it, an' I 'm goin' to send it back.'"

"That 's a likely story!" Mrs. Dansken cried out. "She 'd been trying it on. She had just crammed it back into the box when I went upstairs to call her."

Ann looked at her mistress shrewdly. "Was ye in the room?"

"Of course I was in the room. How did I see the dress if I was n't in the room?"

"Well, ye 'd better have kept out, an' let her have her things to herself. I 'd niver want the missus thrackin' me about. A gurl 's got a right to some place av her own."

"Don't scold me, Ann. I own I was stupid about that — but I tell you, she is a girl who needs watching."

"Ye had me to watch her, an old woman that knows what gurls is. I niver see nothin' wrong wid her, barrin' she 's a bit close about herself; an' it 's what they have to be when they 've got themselves to look out for."

" I thought you hated her."

Ann laughed shortly. "I was none so fond av her at the first off, but whin I see — who 's that goin' out ? "

The street door had closed, somewhat early for the young men to be taking their departure.

" It 's Milly coming back, I should n't wonder," said Mrs. Dansken, listening for a step on the stairs.

" Comin' back? " Ann repeated.

"Yes; did n't you know she was gone ? "

" Wheriver has she gone to, for the good Lord's sake ? " said Ann, rising up. "She tould me she 'd not sleep in this house another night. ' Very well,' says I ; ' wait till I get my kitchen red up an' I 'll go wid. ye to the Sisters'.' An' how long is she gone ? "

" Why, ever so long. I thought she was coming back. Her trunk is here."

. " I 'll jist out, thin, an' afther her. Will ye be gettin' up now? " Ann hesitated, looking at her mistress. Mrs. Dansken saw that she was uneasy.

"Go along, you best old creature! — Ann, wait a minute ! Do you know who sent her the dress? "

"Sure, w'u'd I ask a gurl a thing like that? An' she 'd niver have tould me, anyway."

"I 'm jealous," said Mrs. Dansken, throwing herself back in the bed. "Here you 've been making me believe you despised that girl, and thought about her just the same as I did, and all the while you were on her side."

"No 'm, I 'm none so fond av her," Ann maintained. But she did not wait to "red up" the kitchen. Mrs. Dansken heard the street door again a very few moments after Ann had left her. The young men were laughing over their cigars in the parlor. She put on an apron, entered the dining-room by the hall door, and began to clear the table, keeping the curtain closed, for she did not wish to be questioned. Ann should not find her work waiting for her when she returned from her walk in the dark snowy streets. If Williams had been at home — or if Frank had not gone, how quickly she would trust him now, to go in search of Milly.

Ann walked slowly up and down Harrison Avenue, passing and repassing the windows

of the Clarendon, looking down all the side
streets; finally she ventured to ask one or
two respectable wayfarers if they had seen
a young woman in a dark cloth jacket and
a turban, and carrying a big white box.
Ann was sure the box was in some way
responsible for Milly's giving her the slip.
She meant to cast about in their own neighborhood before taking that long walk across
the town to the Sisters'. She stopped one
of the waiters in the door of the Clarendon
as she passed down on that side of the street.
It was the one whom, without knowing his
nationality, she called the Swedener, who
occasionally brought Mrs. Dansken's orders
for her little festivities. Had he seen Milly
Robinson that evening?

"Yes," the man replied. "She coom mit
a pox; an' she say, leef it in t'e offis for
Mist' Embury. Mist' Embury he coom
shust t'en; unt he say, send t'e pox up to
his room. Unt t'ey walk town street togedder."

Ann gave a grunt. "N-n!" she objected,
in that indescribable form of dissent which
the West has imported from the South.
"That's not Milly Robinson."

" She vas Milly."

" N-n ! " Ann persisted.

" It vas t'e pox, anyhow," the man declared. " I see t'e man vat pack dat pox over to Mis' Dansken, unt he say it vas for Milly."

" Sure I hope it *was* Milly," said Ann, changing her ground of defense. " That 's all I wan' to know. Is she along av our Misther Embury ? "

" She vas mit him. Dey vent town t'e street togedder."

Ann did not go to the Sisters', but she told her mistress that Milly was there ; and Mrs. Dansken was too glad of the assurance to reflect that it was a mile or more to the Sisters' hospital, and that Ann could hardly have gone and returned in the time she had been absent.

" Ye 're to pay her money to me, an' she 'll send for her thrunk in the mornin'."

In her toilsome walk in life Ann had seen many cases of folly and sin end as the case of Milly seemed likely to end, but never one of knightly championship. She had never met with a case of this kind, and out of her experience she drew her conclusions. It hurt her that the girl should have taken herself off without even saying good-by to her old comrade, who had sincerely conquered a prejudice for kindness' sake.

" I doubt but the missus was in the right: she 'd a bad heart, or she 'd niver have give me the slip like that." But, in spite of her own belief, nothing could have induced Ann to destroy the girl's last chance of retreat should the heart not prove so bad after all.

III.

FRANK and Milly were by the bridge again, and this time there was no brown veil between them. Milly's cheeks were not pink like the sunset color on the eastern peaks; they were pale as the snow which starkly outlined them against the night sky. She was awake at last. Frank thought he had never seen a face so beautiful as hers while she told him the story of her wrongs and her insults. Not a word accused him, but he felt that he was responsible for all that had cost her an honorable refuge, a place of safety, if not a home. No doubt he sup-

posed himself to be thinking while he listened to Milly's story and looked at her
beautiful face, but he was merely tingling
with a mixture of passionate promptings.
He scarcely heard what she was saying as
she urged that she must go back, and reminded him for the third or fourth time that
she had come out not expecting to see him,
only to get rid of the dress, which she had
never meant to take.

"And I made you take it. I have
brought all this trouble upon you, Milly;
but, dear, happiness shall come of it. It
was all for the best — to bring us together,
my darling."

"I must go back — I must!" Milly
pleaded.

"You shall never go back," said the
dreamer. "Is it more insults you want?"

"I promised to go back. Ann is going
with me to the Sisters'."

"The Sisters'! Milly, I am the one to
take care of you now."

"No, sir. No, Mr. Embury. You must
n't kiss me — I 'm not — oh, you don't
know, you don't know!"

"Milly," said Frank, "God knows how

we have got where we are — but here we are. We are never going to part any more. Do you understand?"

"I did n't think you 'd say such things to me," sobbed Milly.

"Who, in the name of Heaven, should say such things, if not I? Do you know what I mean?"

"Oh, let me go, sir, please! They 'll be out after me."

"Stop sirring me, will you? Who will be out after you? Is there any one in that house who is likely to care what becomes of you?"

"There 's Ann, sir" —

"Ann be hanged! Can Ann take care of you? Ah, Milly, listen to me! — For Heaven's sake, what is the matter?"

"Look at me!" sobbed the girl, with such wild deprecation in her face that Frank was forced to heed her. "Can't you see?"

"Can't I see? I see that you are a dear, good, helpless girl, who is going to be my wife. We are going to be married to-night. Hush, hush! not a word. — I don't know anything about you? Do you know anything about me? No, I won't hear a word. Can't I see, indeed! I see that you are my darling. There, there! What, more tears, Milly? Am I such a monster?"

"You are good," said Milly. "You are the best — I ever saw; but you don't know — you don't know! Let me go, to-night. Let me tell you — what I said I must."

"You shall tell me all to-morrow. There are things *I* might tell. We will take each other on trust, and I shall get the best of the bargain, my lovely one. Do you know what we are going to do? That poor, in-sulted little gown I made you take — you shall wear it to-morrow night. You will need no chaperone as my wife."

"I can't, I can't!" Milly protested, but no longer with the same force of denial. She struggled in his arms, and he let her go, seeing that some one was approaching.

They were not in a nice part of the town, if any part of it could be called nice after nightfall, when the mountains withdrew their countenances and left it to the light of its flaring windows, its occasional smoky street-lamps and intervals of slippery dark-ness. They were out of the centre of lamps and lighted windows, except the windows of a suburban groggery where a fiddle was tun-

ing up in a crazy way, as if the ear and the
hand went wild that were groping for the
tune. The light of this squalid revelry was
cast upon the foul snow at their feet; it
shone upon the two young faces, pictured
upon the darkness, close together, eye to eye
in the struggle between two wills — one fiery
and undisciplined, and one that was strong,
but sluggish, and sick with fear.

The stranger stared hard, and looked
back as he passed them. He looked back
more than once, and then retraced his steps.
He was a thin, cold-looking man, in a shabby
suit of black, with a pair of dilapidated
" arctics " exaggerating to enormities ·the
size of his feet. He addressed them in a
voice nasal but sweet.

" My young friends, have you found the
Lord? Is he leading you by the hand to-
night ? "

He paused for an answer. " I do not
know the face of this young sister," the
exhorter continued as neither of the young
people spoke; " but, if I am not mistaken,
this young man is Mr. Embury, of the firm
of Williams & Embury — yes ? "

" That 's my name," said Frank. " Are
you a clergyman, sir ? "

"The Rev. Mr. Black, of the Methodist Mission in Second Street. And if you will excuse an old man's advice, Mr. Embury, I think, sir, if this young woman's parents reside in the city, you would better take her home. It is late, my dear young friends, except for such as are out, like myself, upon errands of necessity or mercy."

"Mr. Black," said Frank, "you can do me a very great service, if you will."

Begging Milly to excuse him, he drew the minister aside and spoke with him earnestly, while Milly waited, helplessly sure what this service was likely to be.

"Is the young woman quite satisfied in her mind as to the step she is taking?"

Mr. Black came close to Milly and took her hand, smiling upon her with his intimate, pastoral smile. Milly drew away her hand.

"If she has the least doubt, before it is too late I would advise a talk with my wife — an excellent woman, though I say it, and a woman of great experience where young girls are concerned."

Milly looked repellent. "You don't wish to talk to anybody, do you, Milly?" Frank answered for her. She assented silently.

"Very well; then let us go to my home, and take counsel with our thoughts as we go. And if no objections arise, and you feel that you can trust the state of mind you are in " —

IV.

FRANK had a few moments alone with Milly in the parlor of the parsonage after the ceremony, while Mr. Black consulted with his wife whether it would be possible for them to keep the bride over night.

"I must not take you to the Clarendon to-night, Milly. We cannot have it said around town that I brought you in out of the streets at eleven o'clock at night. I shall take rooms for my wife and come for her the first thing in the morning — my sweet! You won't be lonesome, will you? Does it seem a strange way to take care of you? I want to be so careful of you now, because it had to be so sudden. And this is quite the right sort of place for you to stay."

" I don't want to stay," whispered Milly; " I did n't want to do any of it."

"Oh, please, Milly ! when I must leave

you so soon.   There was nothing else for
us to do, my darling.   If we had not been
meant for each other should we ever have got
where we are ?   I will not believe you don't
care for me — I will make you care ! "

"It 's no use my talking," said Milly,
relenting.   "You do just what you want with
me.   You always did."

"I always intend to — and it shall be just
what my darling likes best."

Mrs. Black, it seemed, could keep Milly
by a little hospitable management.   Milly
made no further objection, and Frank had no
scruples in accepting the obligation.   It is
not unlikely that he felt he was honoring
the parson's dwelling.   While the daughter
made the necessary changes for the night, a
simple entertainment was set forth by the
minister's wife for the young couple who
were beginning their life together under the
roof of strangers, without the blessing of
kith or kin.

Little was eaten and little was said, except by the minister, whose words fell in the
silence without meaning for those they were
intended to encourage and to warn.   Frank
took his leave as soon as possible, kissing

his wife quietly, and commending her, with a look that the minister's wife said was beautiful, to the good woman's care.

She was a woman whose goodness was the most apparent thing about her, except a large forehead and nose that gave a benignant look of authority to her countenance. It was plain that she was mistress of the parsonage, if not of the parson himself. If she had said that he must not marry the young people, he would probably have declined to do so. What she did say, in the brief matrimonial conference in the kitchen before the ceremony was performed, was much to the effect of St. Paul's words on the same question; also, that if "they," meaning her husband, refused to marry them, the young couple could easily find some one else who would.

When Milly had been half an hour alone in the room vacated by the minister's daughter, Mrs. Black went up to her door and knocked. Milly had been sitting on the side of the bed, with her clothes on but in her stocking feet, for her shoes were damp with snow. She had been going back over her poor past, trying to imagine her-

self opening that foolish, blotted page before the eyes of the delicate, imperative
young gentleman who had just bound his
fate to hers for better or for worse.   And
when she looked into the future the prospect
was no surer ; it was impossible to think of
it as *their* future.   She had told the simple
truth when she had said that he could do
what he pleased with her ; but not he nor
any other hero of a girl's fancy could have
power to do away with certain facts which
made this marriage a problem, even to the
slow, unimaginative nature that was dumbly
struggling with it.   When she heard the
heavy step on the stairs and the gentle but
confident knock, Milly could have given a
cry of welcome to this last chance of counsel, if not of escape.

"My dear," said Mrs. Black, coming
promptly to her side, " I came up to see if
you had bed-covers enough — but of course
you can't go to sleep yet," she added, glancing at Milly's dress.   " There's a little fire
in my bed-room, right across the hall.
Would you like to come in and sit awhile?
Mr. Black he's downstairs doing some
writing.   He don't write out his sermons as

a general thing, but this is a letter to a
newspaper, one of our church papers at
home, he 's occasional correspondent for.
They like to know what progress we 're
making here. It 's a wonderful place for
awakenings. It seems when we get right
amongst all that 's blackest and sinfulest in
our poor human nature we find the most
helpfulness, one for another. You 'd be
surprised the rescuer and comforter my
husband 's been able to be, and all because
the work is ready and waiting for any one
who 'll take hold and believe. — Well, dear,
what 's *your* trouble ? We 've all got something. You don't suppose I can't see it is
n't all quite clear before you. How could
it be, poor child ! But he 's a lovely young
man — and you 're very pretty, my dear.
You 've got it all in your own hands."

"It 's no use my being pretty," replied
Milly, despondently. She was sitting in a
low chair by the stove in Mrs. Black's bedroom, forgetting to care that her feet, in
their soiled stockings, were visible. Mrs.
Black was in the big scroll-back rocking-
chair opposite, rocking and talking, and
looking at Milly, not at Milly's stockings,

and snipping her darning threads, without the least confusion of impulses.

"No, not if pretty 's all there is of it. But it 's a good thing when the young man 's so good-looking. It 's best not to have the looks all on his side. Now it ain't because you 're pretty you 're worrying to-night." She examined Milly with her practiced motherly glance. — "My dear, you better go lie down this minute. What have you been through to make you look like that!" She got Milly quickly into her bed and felt her over carefully. "Where do you feel sick?"

"I 'm not sick," said Milly.

"Well, now, out with it, same as if I was your mother! There 's trouble here somewhere."

Mrs. Black waited, holding the girl's hands in her own, looking at her steadily with her mild, strong, dark eyes.

Milly gave a little groan and turned away her face. "Mrs." — She hesitated.

"Mrs. Black," prompted that lady.

"Mrs. Black, I 'm a married woman."

"Of course you are, my dear," said Mrs. Black, with an encouraging squeeze of

Milly's hands. " I was your witness myself, and I 'd uphold you in it, for I saw plain enough that young man was bound to have his way."

" I was married and had a child before I ever saw him."

" And does n't he know you 're a widow ? " Mrs. Black asked, after a silence.

" I 'm not a widow, like any other widow."

" Is n't your husband dead ? "

" Yes, but he left me, first. I never put on black for him, or saw him ; I passed myself off for a girl."

" What did you say, my dear ? "

" I don't know how to tell you what I did. I did n't do anything ; it came of itself somehow, and I let it go on."

" Yes," said Mrs. Black. " It 's the easiest way sometimes. I suspect we 're all inclined that way." She waited for Milly's next words.

" He left me, and I had to come after him. Last spring I got here. I had to come. I was n't to my own home. My home 's in Canada. He took me away from there and he never found me no other home. My father did n't like him, and we were married secret, and I went away with him when it had to be known. My father he's slow, but he's awful stubborn. When I got here I found he'd left me and no word where I was to find him, and then I knew he'd left me for good. And my baby was born at the Sisters' hospital. It died. And when I got strong enough I went to work at Daniel & Fisher's. I told them I was Mrs. Robinson. They did n't understand me, somehow; I suppose they thought I looked young. They called me *Miss* Robinson; and all of a sudden that seemed the easiest way. All those girls in the store were lookin' me over, and talkin' about other girls they knew, and I knew they'd talk that way about me. If I'd said I was Mrs., they'd have wanted to know where was my husband, and I did n't know then he was dead. I was weak and sick and I did n't want to answer questions, and I let it go on. And every day it got harder to get it back."

"My dear, that was a terrible risk you took, besides its being so wrong — though you're punished for it this minute, and I need n't remind you."

"I know it was wrong, Mrs. Black; but

I did n't seem to care, if only I could be let
alone. And nobody knew but the Sisters,
and they 're the same as dead to what 's outside of their own work. But I did n't care,
that 's the truth. I did n't think I was
going to live long, I felt so sick."

"Oh, my! That 's because you never
felt that way before. I don't doubt you felt
miserable enough, my dear; but it ain't so
easy for women to die. We 're dreadful
tough."

"Well, I got better, and I thought I 'd
tell the lady I went to work for, after I left
the store. I left partly for that, so I could
make a fresh start. But I could n't tell her.
Don't you know there 's folks you can't tell
things to and there 's some you can? I could
have told you."

"Well, I 'm just an ordinary woman,"
said Mrs. Black, "and I 've seen such a
sight of trouble. Nothing could ever surprise me."

"I thought perhaps I could tell her, after
a while, when I got used to her; but when I
came to hear her talking I knew I 'd never
tell her. She 'd have had it all over the
house; and when she told things they some-

how sounded different to what they were.
She could make things sound any way she
liked. Ann, the cook she had, found out
I'd had a child. The Sisters told her, and
then I told her the rest. But I did n't
mind Ann. I knew she'd never tell on me.
And after she knew, she was awful good to
me."

"When was it your husband died?"

"It was June when I heard from his
partner that he'd been found. His horse
slipped off the trail and fell on him."

"And you did mourn for him some, I
know!"

"I had my own troubles," said Milly,
sullenly. "It was he brought them on me,
and he never took none of 'em on himself.
He took me away from a good home and he
never give me another."

"Well, you have got trouble now, that's
a fact. But the first thing you've got to do
is to straighten this all out with your husband. You ain't much acquainted, are you?
How did you come to meet with him?"

"He boarded in the house where I was
working."

"Well, surely that shows he ain't got

prejudices. And if he loved you before he knew you 'd had trouble, he won't love you a bit the less now."

"He knew I 'd had trouble, but not — that kind. I know — I tried to tell him. I did try, Mrs. Black!"

"Ah, I 'm afraid you put it off too long, my dear. If you 'd only come to me before the ceremony and told me, I could have made him understand. You 'd have known then how much he thought of you; but it ain't for me to remind you. And now you 're afraid to out with it — ain't that so? Well, I guess he 's human, same 's the rest of us. I can see what he is — headstrong and proud and full of his fine notions, and wants to be loved, like any other man, but dreadful particular who *he* loves. I don't say it 's the safest sort of marriage; but it 's made and done with now, and you 've got your pretty face, and if he ain't sorry for you when you tell him what you 've been through " —

"He 'd be sorry, but — oh, you don't know him!"

"I know we are prone to error, every one of us, as the sparks fly upward. I guess if you were to go back into the history of that young man you'd find he's done things he's wished he had n't done. But it all depends on how much you care for each other. Do you love him, my dear?"

"I don't know," said Milly. "I ain't like myself when I'm with him. He thinks I'm different to what I am, and that makes me different."

"Of course — I see how it is. But it's no use worrying about the future. You know what you've got to do now. You've got to tell him first thing to-morrow morning, and no bones about it! Don't you let him take you in his arms as his wedded wife without your soul is clear before him. If you do, you'll both repent it to the longest day you live."

"I can't ever be his wife, Mrs. Black. That's never going to be. Something will happen to stop it, I know."

"Don't you go to trusting to any such feelings as those. You've trusted and let things go on too much already, my dear; and that's your way, I see. What you need is more confidence. Now don't go to despairing of your marriage. It's begun

badly, but that ain't all your fault. I can
see what chance you had with a young fellow like him. He's got a good deal too
much confidence. But don't you let his confidence be the ruin of you both, and when it
comes to marriages — why, there's all sorts,
and it's amazing how comfortable they turn
out, spite of everything. There's always
marriages just as risky as yours is, when
a new country is being settled up — young
men and women meeting together, with all
sorts of families back of them, so pleased
with all the new ways of seeing one another, and nothing plain and natural to show
'em their inside differences. Why, it's the
greatest wonder in the world they ever make
out as they do, the most of 'em. If you
were to go back in his own family, I guess
you'd find the mates were n't all matches.
It gets evened up somehow, when they come
to live together. There's a blessing, I tell
you, on the relation."

Mrs. Black had indulged a strain of
extreme leniency and hopefulness, to give
Milly courage for her duty. What she said
to her husband, before they slept, was nearer
her true judgment of the case.

"I wish we had n't been the means of it, Samuel. It was mainly my doings, and I 'm punished for thinking they were past reasoning with, both of 'em. I don't know as I ever saw two misguided young creatures in such a fix. I tried to encourage her all I could, but she 's made a miserable piece of work of it so far; and I 'm sorry for him, when he comes to write that letter home."

" And when I saw those two young people in the street," said Mr. Black, " he was the one I took to be the deceiver."

" He 's the kind of deceiver that deceives nobody but himself — and I don't know but that 's as bad as any kind."

"Not in the eyes of the Lord, Martha."

" The Lord can forgive more sins than they two 'll ever commit," said Martha Black, who had a tenderness for the heart that had unburdened itself to her sympathy, and who knew that Milly's troubles had just begun.

Frank's letter to his mother was to have been written before he went to fetch his wife. He rose early for the purpose, after one of those nights of wakefulness we remember for years afterwards as a distinct experience. In his watchings he had composed a number of letters, but when it came to writing them out he got no farther than " Dear Mother." It was to the mother, who takes the brunt of unpleasant family news, he addressed himself. When he had got as far as this he could see his mother's face, he could hear her voice asking his father to step into the library a moment. He could see both their faces as they sat down and looked at each other, with the letter between them. On the whole he concluded to wait until after the ball. He could then tell them of his wife's first appearance in the society of the town, and of her reception.

He had no doubts on this score. It is the men, he theorized, who decide a girl's fate at a ball.

He had changed his small second-story room at the Clarendon for a large one on the first hall, opposite the ladies' parlor. When the arrangement had been concluded at the desk, the clerk remarked that the bridal chamber was coming it rather strong for a single man. Frank flushed, but gave the information with dignity that he had been married the evening before at the Rev.

Mr. Black's, where his wife was now staying.

The clerk smiled the smile of the foolish, and inquired if the lady was any connection of Mr. Black's; and Frank was obliged to relinquish this straw of respectability which he had grasped at for the sake of Milly's antecedents.

Milly had lamented to Mrs. Black, as the chief of her excuses, that she had never had a chance to speak with Frank without fear of interruption, except in the open streets. But now they were alone, for a lifetime, in the bridal chamber of the Clarendon, with window-blinds closed to shut out the staring daylight, with no idea between them of the time, or of how the world was going outside. The world for them had centred in this their first day together.

Frank had bought a belated wedding-ring and was trying it on the finger of his bride.

"You have worn a ring on this finger before," he said, feeling the little depression that encircled Milly's third finger. "What sort of a ring was it? I like to know all about you, how you looked and what you used to wear, before I ever saw you."

This was Milly's opportunity, as if offered her by Heaven. But it had come too suddenly, almost threateningly; she shrunk from it, and the next moment it was gone.

Something within her, perhaps the habit of concealment, confirmed through months of perilous practice, seemed to answer for her, while her stunned conscience listened amazed.

"It was n't a ring I cared for; I took it off because it was too small for me."

After that the day passed hopelessly for her. She was under the spell of her failure, and of Frank's awful unconsciousness..

More and more she felt his standards oppress her. The nameless little refinements of his manner were her despair; she could not meet them out of any social practice in the past, nor with the simplicity of innocence and faith. She longed to escape, back into the miserable muddle of her old life where she had felt at home — anywhere away from this horrible masquerading.

As for Frank, he was the husband now. He was studying his new possession in the light of old, persistent standards — those standards which Milly instinctively feared.

He studied her because he could not get near enough to her to lose himself in her attraction for him. Something clouded the attraction; something undefinable between them that embarrassed him, and balked him of all the allusions, the fond recapitulations, the exchange of ideals and purposes, which should have glorified the day.

She has all that the first woman had, — youth, beauty, purity, and helplessness, — Frank thought, while she dressed for the ball and he gazed at her shyly with beating heart. She is a girl without a family and without a history. Her husband shall give her both.

v.

FRIDAY, the anniversary of the Assembly Ball, was general sweeping-day at Mrs. Dansken's. Ann had taken cold, or so she chose to assert, perhaps as an excuse for an irritability that vented itself in savage excesses of work. Milly's help was wanting, but Ann wrought for both. She worried her tasks, growling like a dog with a bone when her mistress attempted to take a share.

It was matter for curiosity for Mrs. Dansken and for solitary headshakings for Ann
that Milly's trunk still stood in the hall,
a silent postulate, no one inquiring for it,
and no sign of the owner's interest in its
disposal.

"Don't ye be frettin'," said Ann, who
was doing all the fretting herself. "She 'll
not be long parted from her clothes. Belike
she 's sick like meself, with thrampin' thim
snawy streets."

Mrs. Dansken, in the Nile - green silk,
looked and felt every year of her age as
she took her place at table, opposite Hugh
Williams, to give him his late supper. He
had just presented himself, although the
stage had been in an hour. He had not
seen his partner. Mrs. Dansken had the
field to herself, but she took no advantage.
She gave Williams the history of the household during his absence from a point of view
that was magnanimous, considering the sore-
ness of the narrator.

"And where is the girl now?" Williams
asked.

"She is at the Sisters'."

"No, she is n't; because I 've just been

there myself, to make some inquiries about her. I got on the track of that brother of hers — turns out to be her husband." Mrs. Dansken listened with relief and entire conviction to Williams's account of what he had learned about Milly.

"Oh, I shall give Master Frank a dose, if he needs one," he ended. "We 'll have him back here within the week. You don't suppose he could have sent her the gown?"

Mrs. Dansken flouted the idea. "Is it like Frank Embury to be bribing servant girls with cheap finery?" Mrs. Dansken's survey of Frank's purchase had been a hasty and prejudiced one.

"No, of course that 's out of the question," Williams agreed. "She has 'smiled and retreated' with somebody else."

"I 'm not sure about that," said Mrs. Dansken. "Ann insists she is all right — but then, they always stand up for one another."

"I 'm perfectly satisfied, myself," said Williams. "The Sisters had no idea they were giving it away — I 'm keeping you from your party." He looked at his watch.

"Are n't you going?"

"No; I 've done my duty, and it seems there was no hurry after all. And now I 'm going to sleep."

Williams showed the brisk confidence of an ally newly arrived with fresh information on the scene of old complications. Mrs. Dansken was doubtful that the last word had been said; but she knew herself to be helpless, and was glad to leave the matter in his hands.

She was not happy at the thought of meeting Frank, with the difference between them unhealed. The keystone had fallen from the arch of domestic unity. She was no longer sure of the allegiance of her boys. It might transpire that a faction of separatists had secretly been forming in Frank's support; and a revolted favorite has ever been held the most dangerous of private enemies.

It was a relief to find that at half-past nine o'clock — the Assembly assembled early — Frank was not there.

The ladies were all on the floor. Mrs. Dansken noticed the exchange of emphatic looks, the occasional low-spoken words, as they crossed each other's orbits in the dance.

The overstock of young men were whispering and smiling queerly in little knots against the wall. Strode was waltzing with a Mrs. Paul, one of the new ladies in the camp, still under consideration by the other ladies, but entirely acceptable, it seemed, to Mr. Strode. The lady was in a thoroughgoing mood to-night; she neglected even the business of waltzing for energetic conversation with her partner, and seemed impatient of the coolness of his replies.

"He intends to capture the room — take us all by storm." Mrs. Dansken caught these words as the pair swept by her. "Good idea — before you ladies have a chance to combine."

"He's too late, then," said Mrs. Paul. "It does n't take us long, I can assure you, when we 've got a cause."

Strode laughed and stooped to murmur something in her ear, with a glance at Mrs. Dansken.

"Does n't she know?" Mrs. Paul exclaimed aloud. "How very queer! Somebody must tell her at once."

The name of her escort, Mr. Blashfield, was the only one on Mrs. Dansken's card;

but now the waltz was over and she found
herself in the midst of her accustomed circle. She perceived that Strode was crossing
the room with Mrs. Paul, and instantly
fixed her features in an expression of uncon-
sciousnéss until they were at her side, when
she turned in effusive surprise. But Mrs.
Paul proceeded at once to business.

"Mrs. Dansken, have none of these gentlemen told you of the introduction we are
to be favored with to-night? They are very
considerate, I 'm sure, but it 's no time now
to spare one another's feelings. We are to
be taken by surprise, it seems."

"Yes?" said Mrs. Dansken.

"I think it 's perfectly abominable he
should n't have told you! I 'm afraid you
don't look after your young gentlemen, Mrs.
Dansken. You are too busy making them
comfortable."

Allusions to her professional hospitality
were not pleasing to Mrs. Dansken, but she
merely smiled, and asked if it were Mr.
Strode who needed looking after.

"Oh, Mr. Strode can take care of himself, I think. He is n't going to be run off
with by anybody's pretty waitress. It 's

that poor young Embury and your Annie, Allie, whatever her name is: they were married last night — goodness knows where! He's going to present her to us this evening. Do you mean to say you had n't the faintest suspicion what was going on?"

"My dear," said Mrs. Dansken, gallantly hugging to her breast her deep chagrin, "I've had these young persons on my mind all day, especially 'my' Annie, as you call her. I had my suspicions, but I was ashamed of them." She could not help a little huskiness in her voice. "But it seems one need n't be ashamed of anything. I'm happy to say nothing that *girl* could do could possibly surprise me."

"But it is too bad about Frank Embury! And the worst of it is, we can't punish her without punishing him too. I think it's the brazenest performance I ever heard of! The question is, how are we to receive her — as what she is, or what he wants to make us believe she is?" asked Mrs. Paul.

"Oh, I don't care what she is! She is his wife now — let him look out for her." Mrs. Dansken disdained the applause that followed this speech. It was bitter to her that the catastrophe of her household should be paraded in this way, and that a Mrs. Paul should be the one to inform her of it.

" He 's quite capable of it," she went on, her smarting eyes fixed on a far corner of the room. " He has quite circumvented me. I begin to think I 'm a perfect child."

" I don't see why Embury has n't a right to bring his wife. I should want to bring mine, if I had one," said Strode, judicially. " Let them have their dance, I say. Embury has paid for his share of the floor."

" They may have the whole of it for me," said Mrs. Dansken. She asked Blashfield to give her his arm, and he took her away out of the discussion.

" *She 's* all right," commented Mrs. Paul, looking after her. " She will never forgive him — and I would n't either. Any young man may be foolish, but to marry her, and brazen it out to our very faces ! "

" I wish you would take me home," said Mrs. Dansken. " I believe I 'm not much of a fighter after all. Mrs. Paul seems to have taken the whole thing upon her shoulders. She will see that justice is done ; I can't say I care to stay and look on. It will be thumbs down with every woman in the room."

" I ain't anxious to see it myself," said Blashfield. " But don't you think — had n't we better stand by him, Mrs. Dansken? Frank 's a pretty good boy."

Mrs. Dansken gave him a look. "*You* can come back and stand by him, if you wish to. I think you 'll have your hands full."

They were in the middle of the room, opposite the main entrance, when the whisper went round, "There they come!"

Blashfield fairly blenched. He fell back, leaving Mrs. Dansken to face the triumphant young couple, advancing; Embury looking handsomer than she had ever seen him, with a girl on his arm who was the apotheosis of Milly.

All his personal grievances had been outlawed in that day of Frank's seclusion with his wife — the day that had lasted years. He saw Mrs. Dansken before him, as in dreams one sees a friend from whom one has long been separated. He remembered only that she had been kind — that now, if ever, she must be kind. He looked at her earnestly, insistently, imploringly, seeing that her face remained cold. He held out his hand. She swerved from him, and bore off Blashfield with her to a bench against the wall.

"Tell him to come to me one moment — without that girl."

Blashfield obediently crossed the room to the place where Frank had seated his wife. The neighboring ladies had instantly moved away; he was standing at her side, covering her isolation. He had taken her fan and was beating back the bright hair from her temples, not daring to look at her now that the ordeal was upon them.

He could have embraced Blashfield for his bow to Milly and his matter-of-course manner to them both, though the little man was pink with embarrassment. He attempted no foolish congratulations, but asked Milly, quite naturally, if she were well, and said, with a deeper blush, that they missed her awfully.

Milly came out of her stony silence to say, "Mr. Blashfield, would you give my love to Ann, please, and tell her" — A look from Frank disturbed her and she stopped.

"Yes, indeed, Mrs. Embury." Again Frank would have liked to embrace poor Blashfield, who was having a desperate time of it. "Ann is a regular funeral in the house ever since you left. Embury, Mrs. Dansken wants to speak with you. Will you let me stay with Milly?" This was somehow even better than the "Mrs. Embury;" a choking feeling in her throat made Milly put down her head.

"Mrs. Dansken might have spoken to me a moment ago," said Frank. "She did n't seem particularly anxious then."

"She was taken by surprise, you know. You 'd better go and speak to her, Embury. Don't you think he had?" He addressed himself to Milly, who turned her face away and said, "*I* don't want to speak to Mrs. Dansken."

Blashfield looked unhappy. He rose up and bowed again to Milly. "Take her away, for God's sake!" he muttered to Frank, apart. "She has n't a friend in the room."

Frank was cool and savage.

"It would be all right if the women were n't here. But you can't fight women with a woman, you know — and your wife. Take her out of it."

" We 'll have a dance first," said Frank. " But I thank you, Blashfield."

" I 'd like to dance with her myself," said Blashfield, " but I 've got to take Mrs. Dansken home."

" What is the matter with Mrs. Dansken ? "

" She is afraid there 's going to be a row. Come and speak to her, Frank; you ought to, for your wife's sake."

" For my wife's sake ! " Frank echoed scornfully. " I must go back to my wife. Thank you, Blashfield."

" Blashfield is the flag of truce," the ladies said. But the flag of truce disappeared a moment later with Mrs. Dansken, and the ladies understood that the terms of surrender were off.

Frank and Milly took their places as third couple in the lanciers. He had not dared to ask her if she could dance, but she showed no hesitation and bore herself to his entire admiration. The manner of the perfect servant, which Mrs. Dansken had approved, did not forsake her now ; she stood up as calmly as if she had been behind her mistress's chair, with the double file of laughing young men's faces in front of her.

"My brave girl — my beauty," Frank whispered, and the next moment he saw that they were deserted. The set had melted away and they stood in their places alone. He whirled Milly off into another set that was forming; that too dissolved, and left them, objects of commiseration or of derision to the room.

Then they took their seats. "I wish we could go away," Milly said.

"We will go, after a while. I will not skulk out of the room with you and leave a trail of sneers behind us. Who are they? — a lot of washed-out old women; and where did they come from, I should like to know? Ladies don't assemble in mining camps, as a rule." Frank stopped, and Milly said : —

"*I* 'm not a lady. I never pretended to be."

"And they do pretend, that is just the difference." He was more sure of himself, now that the case was simple — his bride to buckler against the world. "We will have one waltz together. Can you waltz, Milly?"

Milly smiled faintly in reminiscence. " What should I care about the music if I 'd never danced to it ? " she asked.

"Ah, that night! Poor Milly! — Heavens, how beautiful you look! You are my Cinderella after all. We 'll make those proud sisters own up who is the belle of the ball. Wait till the men have their turn."

Frank was not himself to-night. He was not in the habit of such speeches as these, but the form of attack he was meeting called forth all that was cruelest and coarsest in his nature. The company had now got down to the level of primitive instincts. It was simply a tussle for supremacy.

When the waltz began Frank rose and took Milly by the hand. Her hand was cold. He looked at her beautiful face and saw that she was colorless, except for her bright hair and her opaque, gem-like eyes, on which the light floated as on dark green water.

" Can you go through with it ? " he whispered.

" Can I waltz? " asked Milly. " You will see."

" What are those poor things going to do

now?" Mrs. Paul exclaimed as they took their places. "Does he imagine that she can dance? I propose we give them the floor."

It was yielded them by tacit consent, and they floated over it, a pair of dancers who might have been chosen to incarnate the spirit of the waltz.

"That 's business," Strode murmured, and then not another word was spoken. The company were reduced to the attitude of mere spectators; every eye following the exalted, dreamlike motions of the beautiful young pair.

This was Milly's triumph. Whether it was worth the cost Frank did not ask himself. He flung himself into it with an aching forecast that such henceforth would be the nature of his wife's triumphs — conquered by strife, and in a field open to all competitors without subtle distinctions. A perfect physical endowment; a sense of rhythm; muscles true to the quiver of a nerve; a "calm, uneager face." The soul of the waltz passed, in anguished ecstasy, before the silent company, and the hearts of the women were pained and the men were at Milly's feet.

But none the less was she doomed.

" Really, one would think it was professional," said Mrs. Paul. "How does she keep herself in practice ? "

" By Jove, she 's stunning ! It does n't look as if she needed much practice," said Strode.

Such remarks did not help Milly's case, especially as a majority of the young men carried their defection to the point of going over to her in a body, asking to be introduced, and crowding her card with their names.

The ladies were beaten from the field. Those who had escorts summoned them, and at eleven o'clock Milly was the only woman in the room.

The best of the men had gone with the ladies. It needed but a glance to show Frank that the tables were turned, and that the retreat of the women had been a stroke of vengeance. The men whose names were on Milly's list were not such as he intended that his wife should dance with.

When it was seen that he was taking his beautiful waltzer away, a crowd of protestants gathered about them, reproaching her familiarly and joking with Frank in a way that drove him wild. Some of them had been drinking. Decidedly Strode was not himself. He had disposed of Mrs. Paul at her door and had hastened back, pausing for a parenthetical glass at the bar, to confirm his indorsement of Milly. It was he who followed up the retreat, who intercepted the pair at the foot of the staircase, and tipsily demanded his dance with the bride. The stairs went up from the office of the hotel, where a crowd of men were laughing witnesses of the scene.

"Some other time, Strode," said Frank, controlling himself.

"Wha' 's your hurry? Have n't you cut her out and got you' brand on her?" Strode muttered, lapsing into cowboy slang.

They had reached the first landing, Strode pursuing. Frank turned upon him. "Clear out, before I kick you downstairs."

Strode braced himself and Frank took him by the collar and flung him backwards off the landing. It was not far to fall. Strode was up and at the bedroom door, sobered and white with rage, as Frank shut the door upon his wife and faced about to meet him.

Strode looked into his eyes. "You 've got to apologize," he muttered.

Frank laughed at this proposition following the scene on the stairs. He was perfectly cool. "Do you want any more of the same sort?" he asked.

"When will you meet me like a gentleman?"

"Like an idiot, you mean! Gentlemen don't fight duels, off the stage."

"Gentlemen, with us, don't use their fists," said the Arkansas boy. "You are a —— coward!"

"Am I? You shall prove it — any ridiculous way you like, and as soon as you like."

"Twelve o'clock, then, out here in the lot back of the hotel. Who 's your friend?"

Frank thought a moment. "Blashfield," he said. "You need n't make a noise about it."

"I think you will squeal first," said Strode.

"Hound!" said Frank, looking after him.

He went into his room and took Milly in his lap, putting his head down upon her shoulder. She laid her hands timidly one on each side of his temples, and felt the hot veins throbbing.　Her heart was very soft towards him, her wonderful young lover, her protector, whom she found more formidable than all the dangers he had tried to save her from.

"He'd taken too much, had n't he?" she whispered.

Frank shuddered.

"You ain't afraid he'll make you trouble?"

He shook his head.　He gripped her to him, gave her a little shake, and put her down from his knees.

"Why would n't you let me dance?" she asked presently, following him with her eyes as he strode about the room.　"You was n't jealous, was you?"

He threw up his head like a creature that feels itself stifling.　It was clear that Milly had not perceived the nature of her success, and was immensely supported by it.　Her exhilaration was even more dreadful to him than the incomprehension he had been beating himself against all day.

"Milly," he said, "did I ever show you my mother's picture?"

"Is it that one in a leather frame on your bureau?"

Again, was it possible he could be sensitive on so slight a point as that Milly should be already intimate with his personal belongings in her domestic capacity? "Yes," he said, with a sigh. Once he had compared this beautiful girl to Enid, who was so sweet and serviceable, and had sympathized with Geraint in his desire to "kiss the tender little thumb that crossed the trencher as she laid it down;" though as a matter of fact Milly's thumb was neither little nor tender, and she had been instructed by Mrs. Dansken never to let it cross the trencher.

"My mother was never anything but kind to any living soul, I believe. Do you think you could be fond of her, Milly? Have you looked at her face?"

"Yes," said Milly, listlessly. "She looks older," — she hesitated, — "but that, maybe, is the way she's dressed."

"The way she is dressed? Why, how should she be dressed?" Did Milly suppose his mother wore her hair in a fuzz on her forehead, like Mrs. Dansken, and dressed in Nile-green silk? Then he remembered that the picture had been taken when she was in mourning. But it did not matter. He felt

as if he should never speak of his mother
again.

Milly was silent, feeling that she had
missed the right words, as usual. She had
not been thinking much of what she was
saying. She had not got as far as Frank's
mother yet. Frank saw that she had sunk
into that attitude of stolid watchfulness,
with something reproachful in it, that all
day had been his despair. Her triumph was
cold. He looked at her, fair as she was,
with a face of that simple but elusive type
the masters felt for, with broad, soft touches,
in palest chalks, on the margins of bolder
conceptions; he thought of Andrea del
Sarto, of Lydgate, of all the men who had
wrecked their lives in such frail craft as this.
He thought of that nameless youth who was
surprised and stabbed as he stepped from
a gondola after a night's delirious drifting
— the youth who boasted that he had
" lived." But he could not find the comfort of a prototype, either in romantic reality or in realistic romance. He was no
Andrea, no Lydgate; he was not even a
youth who had " lived ; " he was merely the
husband of Milly. As for the duel, it was

of a piece with all the rest. Last night he
had married Milly; to-night, driven by the
same fantastic chain of tragic common-
places, he was to fight a duel for her sake;
or to go through the form. He most certainly did not intend to hit Strode, and he
doubted on general principles that Strode
would be able to hit him, should the affair
culminate in their pointing pistols at each
other.

At a quarter to twelve Blashfield came to
the door. "Strode will apologize," he said,
"if you will give him a chance."

"I 'll give him every chance when we get
on the ground."

"He is downstairs now. He has come to
himself. There 's no sense in this meeting,
you know."

"What do you want of me? It 's a quarter to twelve now. Let him meet me where
he said he would and we will shake hands.
No, I won't go downstairs, Blashfield. I
shall punch his head if I do."

"Are you going to be reasonable?"

"I have been reasonable. Strode was
tipsy. Let him say so, when the time comes,
and ask my pardon. I 'm not going to hunt
him up."

"I 'll bring him up here."

"Thank you, I 've no use for him up here. Keep an eye on him, Blasshy, if you 're afraid he won't stay with it."

"He is n't my man."

"Keep with him all the same. I 'll meet you at the barber's."

The quarter-hour was passed. Frank had said to Milly that he would have to go out for a few moments ; it was the little engagement he had told her he would have to sit up for. He would tell her about it and make her laugh, when he returned. He himself laughed as he kissed her.

He was leaving the hotel when he met Hugh Williams, beaming with outstretched hand.

"The dance lets out early to-night," he remarked pleasantly. "I did n't know Mrs. Dansken was at home until I stumbled over Blashfield."

Frank decided, after a look at Williams, that Blashfield had kept the meeting quiet.

"Well, how 's everything since I 've been away? I 've been asleep for two hours. Mrs. Dansken gave me some supper — and, by the way, I 'm mightily pleased that girl

has gone." Williams had concluded to give
Frank his "dose" while he could speak
without apparent knowledge of all that had
taken place in his absence, since it would
never do to let Frank suppose he had been
talked over.

"What girl?"

"Come out here, Frank," said Williams;
and when they were in the street he said,
"You know who I mean — the Perfect
Treasure. I met the partner of her brother.
The brother turns out to be a husband. He
was n't a particularly good one, it seems,
and so she hedges a little and calls him " —

"It 's a lie."

"I thought it was a lie myself, Frank."
Williams would not look at his friend to see
how he was taking it. "I 'm not much in
the habit of packing lies about, especially
lies about a woman, so I stepped round to
the Sisters'," he went on, trying to speak
naturally and in an unpremeditated way —
"who took care of her, you know, when her
child was born " —

Frank clutched him by the shoulders.
"Stop!" he panted, "you are talking about
my wife."

The two men reeled apart and stared at each other.

"Curses on it, why did n't you tell me?"

"Why did you open on me, before I could speak? Out with it now, to the last word!"

"I have nothing to say about your wife, Frank."

"I 'll have it out of you, I say."

Blashfield, who had been waiting for his principal, caught sight of him and joined them. He gripped him by the elbow. "Do you know what time it is?" he suggested.

"I 'll be with you in a moment, Blashfield; I want to speak with Williams — I 'll be around."

Blashfield gave his arm another squeeze and ran off to the rendezvous.

"Frank," said Williams, "I can't take those words back, but you should allow for my ignorance. I 've been gone a thousand years, it seems."

"You can say you believe me when I tell you those words are false."

Williams did not speak.

"Your silence, do you know, is insulting."

"I have nothing to say about your wife,

Frank," Williams repeated, "except that she is a very handsome girl and I hope you will be happy."

" It is kind of you to mention her beauty."

" I think we had better not talk any more to-night. There 's all to-morrow, you know."

" I have no desire to talk, but I think there is something more for you to say."

" What is it? "

" You will finish what you began to tell me, and then you will say whether you believe it is true."

" What does it matter what I believe? Go to your wife and find out the truth."

" Go to my wife, and ask her if she has had a child ? "

" God help you, Frank. Go to her and learn to know your wife ; and be thankful, whatever she is, that she is no worse. You 've got to know the truth, sooner or later. It 's all over the camp to-night."

" What is the truth ? "

" Go to her, man. Don't ask me. For God's sake, am I to tell you she has been a mother ; that her child was born at the hospital ; that its father deserted her before it was born ? I 'd have kept it from you with my life, but I told Mrs. Dansken two hours ago, before she went to the ball. It's all over the town by now, God forgive me!"

Frank could not have been sure that he heard the last words of his friend, or that he was the man who was being led up and down the street, brokenly, like one drugged or intoxicated.

The rage had all gone out of him, the flame that had driven him for the past five days, since the evening he was published before the household. In its place was a light-headed calmness, in which he could think of Milly with a strange indifference.

"Have you got any money about you?" were the first words he said.

"Any money?" said Williams. "Do you want money to-night?"

"Yes, I want some money. I want a good deal. Do you know it's my wedding night?"

Williams stopped him in the street and fairly shook him, to get his attention.

"Frank, do you mean she is n't your wife yet?"

"Yes, she's my wife. I was married last night."

" Then, it is too late " —

" Too late to desert her ? She 's been deserted once, you say ? "

Williams groaned, and they resumed their aimless walk.

" Did you say you had n't any money in your clothes ? "

" I 've got two dollars and a half."

" Don't get excited," said Frank ; " I 'm not out of my head. I 'm going upstairs a moment. You need n't follow me. Can't a man speak to his wife ? "

He went up swiftly to the door of his room. There was something he had yet to do ; it was rather a crazy thought, but it chimed in with his fancy that he must not be ungentlemanly, whatever he meant by that. He stood a moment listening by the door. The room was quiet. Could she be asleep on her wedding night — his bride without a history ; the girl who within the year had suffered, in poverty and desertion, the agony of motherhood ; who had buried her child ; who had waltzed in his arms that night, a spectacle — how had he paraded his shame ! This was why the ladies had retreated and the men had stayed, those who were suited to the company of his bride.   He prayed that she might be asleep.

Milly had been lying dressed and awake on the bed when she first heard her husband's step, and knew that the moment she had been drifting upon had come, and that she must meet it at last with her lamp unlighted and the darkness of falsehood in her soul.   She wondered if it might be possible for her to speak even now; but as Frank approached the bed the instinct of dread alone prevailed, and she lay still, scarcely breathing, and trembling like a hare in its form.

He stooped over her and thought that she slept; but with that horrible weak yet heavy beating of the heart going on inside his breast he would not have known if it had been death he looked upon, instead of sleep. In the hollow of her arm that was nearest him he deposited all the gold and silver he could find in his pockets, softly, one piece laid against another, not to waken the sleeper. He did not despoil himself further. His watch and the ornaments that completed his dress he kept upon his person.   He looked at her once more, her face turned

away from the little heap of coin gleaming
against the whiteness of her arm. The sight
smote him, and yet what more did he owe
her now?

Williams watched him as he came through
the office. He stopped at the bar and asked
for a glass of brandy; he drank it and then
went over to the desk and spoke to the clerk,
saying something about feeling the brandy
in his head. His behavior struck Williams
as simply idiotic under the circumstances,
unless the boy had some purpose in making
a fool of himself. He caught sight of Williams and smiled in a way that did not allay
his friend's uneasiness. Hugh took him by
the arm and said, speaking low as they stood
by the door together : —

"This is n't fair to her, Frank. You
ought to give her a chance to explain."

"She can't explain now," said Frank,
lightly. "She 's asleep. And I have an
engagement. Will you go up there and
wait till I come back? The room is the
one opposite the ladies' parlor. Stay round
where you can hear her if she calls."

"Where in the world are you going? I
don't like your engagement at twelve o'clock
at night."

"A man can't help his engagements," said Frank. "You heard me promise Blasshy I'd be there. You were pretty rough on her, Hugh. You owe her a good turn. And if your friend's wife is n't all you'd like her to be, is that any reason you should n't stand by her?"

"I should prefer just now to stand by you."

"So you will, if you 'll just wait, you know. Wait up there till I get back."

"Go on, then; I will wait; and don't be out all night."

Frank smiled back at his friend with that wretched, inconsequent smile.

Hugh was still uneasy, but the fact that Blashfield was concerned with Frank's engagement comforted him somewhat: his friend could not have any very desperate or tragic intentions with Blasshy in tow.

The ladies' parlor was empty, but Williams was too restless to compose himself to solitary contemplation of its splendors. He walked the length of the hall, back and forth, pausing once at Milly's door when he thought he heard a sound of weeping. "Poor little fool," he said to himself, "I could be sorry for her if it were not for Frank — his life spoiled at twenty-four."

He stood in one spot in the middle of the hall for some moments, thinking of his friend's future.

" And what is he up to now, I wonder? " He looked at his watch and saw that Frank had been gone three quarters of an hour.

A window at the lower end of the hall was open and the wind blew harshly in, making the lamps flicker. He stepped down the hall to close it, and as the keen night air crossed his face he heard the report of a pistol. He went to the window and looked out. It was a high window, opening on the narrow fenced alley between the hotel kitchen and the open lot behind. The alley was lighted for a short distance by the lamps of late workers in the kitchen ; beyond, as far as he could see in the direction of the shot, all was dark.

Williams found the door of a back stairway and ran down to a rear entrance opening upon the fenced passage. One or two of the hotel servants — there were but few up at that hour — stood bareheaded in the alley, in the light from the hot kitchen, staring into the blackness of the lot.

" What is it ? " Williams asked.

"Some young fellows went by here a while back," one of the waiters said, peering ahead of him. "I do' know what they 're up to."

Williams crowded past him and met Blashfield, a few steps farther on, running, his face towards the light.

" Who is hurt ? " asked Williams, seeing that something was wrong.

" Embury."

" How — who did it ? "

Blashfield did not answer, but ran on. He gave money to one of the waiters, who disappeared and himself took the nearest way into the street.

Williams ran blindly forward towards a spot of light near the rear fence of the lot. There were figures moving against it ; those nearest the light were motionless, but one was moving back and forth in a curious trot. A few steps brought Williams near enough to see that it was Strode, still in evening dress except that he had changed his coat for a reefing jacket. He grasped Williams by the hand and began a childish babbling. Hugh could not shake him off ; he ran beside him talking excitedly.

"I thought you were the sheriff. I'm waiting to give myself up; but the boys will tell you, Williams, I never meant to fight. I had n't a thing against him. I offered to apologize. I was n't even heeled. The boys will tell you one of 'em had to lend me a pistol; I had n't a weapon on me."

"Let go of me, Strode. Where is he?"

"I'm taking you there. He was bound to have the thing come off. You can ask the boys if I could help myself. I don't know how I came to hit him. I never meant to do it. And he never fired a shot. His pistol was cold. I think he was drunk, Williams, or else he's off his head. Why, good Lord, it was nothing — what I said."

The figures by the spot of light moved aside and showed one that lay on the snow, in an angle of the fence, sheltered from the wind. A lantern at his feet shone upward upon his blanched hands and chin and throat.

"How are you now, Embury?" asked Strode, pressing up. "You ain't much hurt, are you?"

Hugh put him aside. "Where is it, Frank?" he said. "Are you bleeding much?"

Frank groaned as Hugh passed his hand over the soaked clothing, feeling for the wound.

" It was the brandy," he muttered. " You saw me take it, Hugh. Went to my head like — keep them off a minute," he whispered.

" Has Blashfield gone for a doctor ? " Hugh inquired.

" Yes," he was told. " We thought we had n't better move him."

" Well, step away, boys, a moment, will you? O Frank, I could curse myself to death, if that would save you ! "

" I 've got what I wanted. You 'll hush up the talk, Hugh ? Let them think it was the brandy — went to my head," he murmured wanderingly.

" Is there anything else, dear boy ? You 'll get a chill lying here."

" No — I wanted to tell you — I 've got what I wanted," Frank repeated dreamily. " You must not think — that you " — He sighed, and gave up the effort to explain. " It was not happy," he whispered, trying to fix his eyes upon his friend's face. They could not hold the look ; the meaning faded out of them, and he spoke no more.

"We must get him in," said Hugh. They laid him on an overcoat stretched upon the snow, and carried him in, past the lights of the kitchen, by the servants' entrance.

"Not upstairs," Hugh whispered.

They turned into the dining-room, where the tables were set in order again for the morning, and laid him on the floor with a pile of cheap quilts from one of the waiters' beds beneath him.

.   .   .   .

The doctor had gone, commanding that Frank should not be moved, his slender chance for life depending on absolute quiet.

It was a Leadville night, wind and sharp volleys of sleet succeeding the early hours of still darkness. From time to time the watchman came in and put coal, noiselessly, with his mittened hands, upon the fire.

Frank had not spoken since his fainting-fit when they carried him in. Towards morning he opened his eyes and turned them upon Hugh, with that look which those who have watched by the dying recognize as the approach of the final change — the look that obliterates personality, that makes the young face old and the old face young.

Hugh saw that he wished to speak. He gave him the stimulant the doctor had ordered in case of a return to consciousness, and waited for its effect.

"Could you go up softly, before she wakes, and take that money away?" Frank whispered.

Hugh thought that he was wandering. Presently he said, quite collectedly, "When you take me home, tell them everything. Perhaps they will not mind, if they know — I got what I wanted."

"Oh, my dear boy, was there no way out of it but this?"

"Not for me — the way of the foolish," he murmured.

But at the last, the smile that dawned upon the still face was an awesome sight to see. Williams thought, as he dwelt and dwelt upon it, and tried to strengthen his faith and ease his pain by gazing, that if Frank's father and mother could but see that look, there must have been consolation, even for them, in that marvelous light shed by the unknown upon this wreck of the known.

When the smile, with its silent protest

against grieving, had been put away out of sight, Hugh's pain returned ; he saw all the wasted moments of retrieval, all the turning-points that had been hurried past.

Mrs. Dansken showed him a letter she had written to Frank's mother, bitterly accusing herself and giving minute details.

" You have n't said anything about what I did," said Hugh, when he had read the letter.

" You did nothing that I was not responsible for."

" You can't tell the whole truth about this matter, Mrs. Dansken. Better leave it alone. I will tell them all that he wanted them to know."

" But they will never know his provocation."

" They know their own boy — and would it comfort them to think we had muddled his life away here among us? You can't tell the whole truth, Mrs. Dansken. We don't know it ourselves."

There have been dancers and dancing on the floor of the Clarendon dining-room since the night of Milly's début, but very few of the original Assembly ever appeared there again in pursuit of pleasure.

There was one corner of the room, over against the bench where Milly had sat at bay, that was haunted for those who helped to lay the young bridegroom there upon the floor, as it might have been, at her feet. Milly herself never entered the room again, nor willingly looked in the face one of those who witnessed her entrance and her exit there. Six months after that evening, the household at No. 9 had dispersed and knew each other no more except by hearsay.

Blashfield continued on his amiable career westward until he reached Honolulu, where he married an heiress of the island, with a shade, it is said, of the liberally disseminated blood of the royal family in her veins. She is reported to be a beautiful woman, with a yard or more of darkest brown hair, and a constitutional leaning towards the wearing of wrappers in the afternoon.

Mrs. Dansken continued to make Hugh Williams the confidant of her grief and repentance for the miscarriage of her relations with Embury; but in respect to Milly she could never be brought to accuse herself except for the fact of the girl's presence in the house. With no audience to applaud, Hugh ceased to try to make points against her in conversation. Before a year had passed he was the sole boarder at No. 9, and this time the arrangement was a permanent and an exclusive one. Mrs. Dansken was a few years older than her philosophical husband, but his was the elder temperament. Hugh had parted with his best hopes in the way of marriage some time before he made the acquaintance of his Leadville landlady : he had always liked the merry, capable, honest little woman ; he used to feel her wearinesses, her mistakes, and humiliations almost as if they had been his own ; he did not mind her sharp tongue or her rowdy little ways, and she made him, he believed, a better comrade in his wandering Western life than a delicately bred, supersensitive, romantic girl from the more carefully weeded ranks of society. But it was long since he had known any girl of this sort, and his ideas on the subject were somewhat vague.

Strode went to New Mexico, where the story of his having killed his man in a duel after a Leadville dance had preceded him, and won for him prestige of a kind which, under the circumstances, he did not covet. He never had occasion to confirm the report that described him as a dead-shot and a dangerous man in a quarrel.

Milly went to live with Mrs. Black, who, with her gift for discerning what was best in those around her, discovered that Milly was " a born sick-nurse " — of the capable and restful, rather than the intuitive, kind. There was plenty of employment outside of the hospitals for Milly's powers during the succeeding season at the camp. Sometimes it was the mother of a young babe at some crazy cabin on a claim that the father was " holding down," perhaps with barricade and shotgun ; sometimes a houseful of little children prostrated by an epidemic. Once it was a traveler overtaken at his hotel — a big stock-raiser from Montana, in beaver overcoat and diamond pin, who perforce upon his recovery presented his pretty nurse with the life he was pleased to owe to her services. What Milly did with the gift, after she went back with him to his cattle-ranch, is not known. But Mrs. Black was glad to have the girl off her mind, she said. " For a girl as pretty as that, who has n't learned to say either yes or no, is n't safe to have around in a place where there are so many men folks."

Poor Frank, alas ! had given occasion for all the family prophets who had ever doubted him to say, " I told you so." But there is one little girl who will always believe that if they had only allowed her to marry her own love all would have been so different. Perhaps a belief of this kind is a better thing than its realization could have been ; at all events, Mr. and Mrs. Mason still think that they knew best.

THE FATE OF A VOICE.

THERE are many loose pages of the earth's history scattered through the unpeopled regions of the Far West, known but to few persons, and these unskilled in the reading of Nature's dumb records. One of these unread pages, written over with prehistoric inscriptions, is the cañon of the Klamath River.

An ancient lava stream once submerged the valley. Its hardening crust, bursting asunder in places, left great crooked rents, through which the subsequent drainage from the mountain slopes found a way down to the desert plains. In one of these furrows, left by the fiery ploughshare, a river, now called the Klamath, made its bed. Hurling itself from side to side, scouring out its straitened boundaries with tons of sand torn from the mountains, it has slowly widened and deepened and worn its ancient channel into the cañon as it may now be seen.

No one can tell how long the river has been making the bed in which it lies so restlessly. Riding towards it across the sunburnt mountain pastures, its course may be traced by the black crests of the lava bluffs which line its channel, showing in the partings of the hills. From a distance the bluffs do not look formidable ; they seem but a step down from the high, sunlit slopes, an insignificant break in the skyward sweep of their long, buoyant lines. But ride on to the brink and look down. The bunch-grass grows to the very edge, its slight spears quivering in light against the cañon's depths of shadow. The roar of the river comes up to your ears in a continuous volume of sound, loud or low, as the wind changes. Here and there, where the speed of the river has been checked, it has left a bit of white sand beach, the only positive white in the landscape. The faded grasses of the hills look pale against the sky [it is a country of cloudless skies and long rainless summers] — only the dark cañon walls dominate the intensity of its deep unchanging blue. The broad light rests, still as in a picture, on the fixed black lines of the bluffs, on the slopes of wild pasture whose curves flatten and crowd together as they approach the horizon. A few black dots of cattle, grazing in the distance, may appear and then stray out of sight over a ridge, or a broad-winged bird may slowly mount and wheel and sink between the cañon walls. Meanwhile, your horse is picking his way, step by step, along the bluffs, cropping the tufts of dry bunch-grass, his hoofs clinking now and then on a bit of sunken rock, which, from the sound, might go down to the foundations of the hills ; there are cracks, too, that look as if they went as deep. The basalt walls are reared in tiers of columns with an hexagonal cleavage. A column or a group of columns becomes dislocated from the mass, rests so, slightly apart ; a girl's weight might throw it over. At length the accumulation of slight, incessant, propelling causes overcomes its delicate poise ; it topples down ; the jointed columns fall apart, and their fragments go to increase the heap of débris which has found its angle of repose at the foot of the cliff. A raw spot of color shows on the weather-worn face of the cliff, and beneath it a shelf is left, or a niche, which the tough sage and the scented wild syringa creep down to and fearlessly occupy in company with straggling tufts of bunch-grass.

One summer a party of railroad engineers made their camp in the river cañon, distributing their tents along the side of a gulch lined with willows and wild roses, up the first hill above it, and down on the white sand beach below. The quarters of the division engineer, who had ladies with him in camp that summer, the tents of the younger members of the corps, the cook-tent, and the dining-shed made a little settlement by themselves on the hill; while the camp of the "force" was lower down the gulch. Work on that division of the new railroad had been temporarily suspended, and the engineer in charge, having finished his part of the line to its junction with the valley division, was awaiting orders from his chief.

It was September, and the last week of the ladies' sojourn in camp. They were but two, the division engineer's wife and the wife's younger sister, a girl with a voice. No one who knew her ever thought of Madeline Hendrie without thinking of her voice, a fact she herself would have been the last

to resent. At that time she was ordering her
life solely with reference to the demands of
that imperious organ. An obstinate huskiness which had changed it since the damp, late
Eastern spring, and had veiled its brilliancy,
was the motive that had sent her, with her
sister, to the dry, pure air of the foot-hills.
In the autumn she would go abroad for two
or three years' final study.

It was Sunday afternoon in camp. Since
work on the line had ceased there was little
to distinguish it from any other afternoon,
except that the little Duncan girls wore
white dresses and broad ribbons at lunch
instead of their play frocks, and were allowed to come to the six o'clock dinner in
the cook-tent. Mrs. Duncan had remarked
to her husband that Madeline and young
Aldis seemed to be making the most of their
farewells. They had spent the entire afternoon together on the river beach, not in
sight of the camp, but in a little cove se-
cluded by willows, where the brook came
down. Mrs. Duncan could see them now
returning with lagging steps along the shore,
not looking at each other and not speaking,
apparently. The rest of the camp was on
its way to dinner.

"I told you how it would be, if you brought her out here, you know," Mr. Duncan said, waiting for his wife to pass him, with her skirts gathered in one hand, along the foot-bridge that crossed the brook to the cook-tent.

"Oh, Madeline is all right," she replied.

But Aldis was missing at table, and Madeline came down late, though without having changed her dress, and during dinner avoided her sister's eye.

"You 're not going out with him again, Madeline!" Mrs. Duncan found a chance to say to the girl after dinner, as she was hurrying up the trail with a light shawl on her arm. "*All* the afternoon, and now again! What can you be thinking of?"

Mrs. Duncan could see Aldis walking about in front of the tents on the hill, evidently on the watch for Madeline.

"I must," she said hurriedly. "It is a promise."

"Oh, if it has come to *that*" —

"It has n't come to anything. You need not be troubled. To-night will be the last of it."

"Màdeline, you must not go. Let me

excuse you to Aldis. I cannot let you go till I 've had a chance to talk with you."

"That is what I have promised *him* — one more chance. You cannot help us, Sallie. Go back, dear, and don't worry about me."

These words were hastily whispered on the trail, Aldis walking about and gloomily awaiting the result of this flying conference between the sisters. Mrs. Duncan went back to the house only half-satisfied that she had done her duty. It was not the first time she had found it difficult to do her duty by Madeline, when it happened to conflict with the inclinations of that imperative youngest daughter of the house of Hendrie. However, it was not for Madeline that she was troubled.

The path leading to the bluffs was one of the many cattle-trails that wind upward, with an even grade, from base to summit of every grass-covered hill on the mountain ranges. Madeline and Aldis shortened the way by leaving the trail and climbing the side of the bluff where it jutted out above the river. It was a steep and breathless struggle upward, and Madeline did not refuse the accustomed help of her companion's hand, offered in silence with a look which she ignored.

Mechanically they sought the place where it had been their custom to sit on other evenings of the summer they had spent together, — one of those ledges a few feet from the summit of the bluff, where part of a row of columns had fallen. Cautiously they stepped down to it, along a crevice slippery with dried grasses, he keeping always between her and the brink.

The sun had already set to the camp, but from their present height once more they could see it drifting down the flaming west. Suddenly, as a fire-ship burns to the water's edge and sinks, the darkening line of the distant plains closed above that intolerable splendor. All the cool subdued tones of the cañon sprang into life. The river took a steely gleam. Up through the gate of the cañon rolled the tide of hazy glory from the valley, touched the topmost crags, and mounted thence to fade in the evening sky. The two on the bluffs sat in silence, their faces pale in the deepening glow, but Madeline had crept forward on the ledge, nearer to Aldis, to look down. It was the first confiding natural movement she had made towards him since the shock of this new phase of their friendship had startled her. Aldis was grateful for it, while resolved to take all possible advantage of it. At his first words she drew back, and he knew, before her answer came, that she had instantly resumed the defensive.

"Everything has been said, except things it would be unkind to say. Why need we go over it all again?"

"That is what we came up here for, is it not? To go over it all once more and get down to the very dregs of your argument."

"It is not an argument. It is a decision, and it is made. There is nothing more I can say, except to indulge in the meanness of recrimination."

"Go on and recriminate, by all means! That is what I want, — to make you say everything you have on your mind. Then I shall ask you to listen to me. What is it that you are keeping back?"

"Well, then, was it quite honest of you to seem to accept the conditions of our — being together this summer, as we have been, and all the while to be nursing this — hope, —for me to have to kill? Do you think I enjoy it?"

" The conditions ? " he repeated. " What conditions do you mean ? I knew you intended yourself for a public singer."

The girl blushed hotly. " Why do you say 'intended myself'? I did not choose my fate. It has chosen me. You must have known that marrying " — the word came with a kind of awkward violence from her lips — "anybody was the last thing I should be likely to think of. A voice is a vocation in itself."

" I did not propose marriage to you as a vocation. As for that hope you accuse me of secretly harboring, I have never held you responsible for it. I took all the risks deliberately when I gave myself up to being happy with you, and trying to make you happy with me. You have been happy sometimes, have you not?"

" Yes," she confessed ; "too happy, if this is the way it is to end."

"But it is not? Perhaps I ought to thank you for being sorry for me, but that is not what I want. I want to make you sorry for yourself, and for the awful mistake you are making."

" Oh, the whole summer has been a mistake! And this place and everything have been fatal! But if you had only been honest with me, it might have all been different. I should have been on my guard."

"Thank heaven you were not! Do you suppose the man lives who would put a girl on her guard, as you say, and endure her company on such terms?"

"You know what I mean. I am not free; I am not — eligible. I thought you understood that and admitted it. We were friends on that basis."

"I never admitted anything of the kind or accepted any basis but the natural one. When you make your own conditions for a man and assume that he accepts them, you should ask yourself what sort of an animal he is. Most of us believe we have an inalienable right to try to win the woman we have chosen, if she is not bespoken or married to another man."

"I am bespoken then. Thank you for the word. My life is pledged to a purpose as serious as marriage itself. You need not smile. Love is not the only inspiration a woman's life can know. I shall reach far more people through my art than I could by just living for my own preferences."

" You still have preferences, then ? "

" Why should I deny it. I don't call it
being strong to be merely indifferent. I
can care for things and yet give them up.
I don't expect to have a very good time
these next three years. I dare say I shall
have foolish dreams like other girls, and look
back and count the time spent. But what
I truly believe I was meant to do, that I
will do, no matter what it costs. There is
no other way to live. Listen ! " — she
stopped him with a gesture as he was about
to speak. She raised her head. Her gray
eyes, which had more light than color in
them, were shining with something that
looked like tears, as she gave voice to one
long, heart-satisfying peal of harmony, pro-
longing it, filling the silence with its rich
cadences, and waking from the rocks across
the cañon a faint eerie repetition, an echo
like the utterance of a voice imprisoned in
the cliff. " There," she said, " are the two
me's, the real me and what you would make
of me — the ghost of a voice — an echo of
other voices from the world I belonged to
once, calling in the wild places where you
would have me buried alive."

He smiled drearily at this girlish hyperbole. " I think there is room here even for a voice like yours. It need not perish for want of breath."

" No, but for want of listeners. I could not sing in an empty world."

" You would have one listener. I could listen for ten thousand."

" Oh, but I don't want you. I want the ten thousand. There are plenty of women with sweet voices meant for only one listener. You should find one of those voices and listen to it the rest of your life." There was a tremulous, insistent gayety in her manner which met with no response. " As for me," she continued, " I want to sing to multitudes. I want to lean my voice on the waves of great orchestras. I want to feel myself going crazy in the choruses, and then sing all alone in a hush — oh, don't you know that intoxicating silence? It takes hundreds to make it. And can't you hear the first low notes, and feel the shudder of joy? I can. I can hear my own voice like a separate living thing. I love it better than I love myself! It is n't myself. I feel sometimes that it is a spirit that has trusted itself to my keeping. I will not betray it, even for you."

This little concession to the weakness of human preference escaped her in the ardor of her resolve. It was not lost upon Aldis.

"Do you think I wish to silence you," he protested. " I love your voice, but not as a separate thing. If it is a spirit, it is your spirit. But I could dispense with it, easily !"

" Of course you could. You don't care for me as I am. You have never admitted that I have a gift which is a destiny in itself. If you did, you would respect it ; you could not think of me, mutilated, as I should be if you took away my one means of expression."

" Oh, nobody who has anything to express is so limited as that. Besides, I would n't take it away. I would enlarge it, not force it into one channel. I would have the woman possess the voice, not the voice possess the woman. I should be the last to deny that you have a destiny ; but I have one too. My destiny is to love you and to make you my wife. There is nothing in that that need conflict with yours."

" I should think there was everything !"

" You have never let me get so far as a single detail, but if you will listen."

" I thought I had listened pretty well for

one who assumes that it is her mission to be heard," Madeline again said, with a piteous attempt at lightness, which her hot cheeks and anxious eyes belied.

"Granting that it is your mission, this part of the world is not so empty as it looks. The people who would make your audiences here are farther apart than in the cities, but they have the enthusiasm that makes nothing of distance. They would make pilgrimages to hear you — whole families in plains-wagons with the children packed in bed-quilts. And the cowboys! they would gather as they do to a grand round-up. It would be a unique career for a singer," he continued ignoring an interruption from Madeline, asking who would evoke this widespread enthusiasm, and whether he would have her advertised in the "Wallula News Miner."

"There would be no money in it for us." (Madeline winced at the pronoun.) "I would not have your lovely gift peddled about the country. There would be no floral tributes or press notices you would care for, or interviews with reporters or descriptions of your dresses in the papers. You might never have the pleasure of seeing your picture in the back of the monthlies, advertising superior toilet articles; but to a generous woman who believes in the regenerating influence of her art, I should think there would be a singular pleasure in giving it away to those who are cut off from all such joys. I know there are singers who boast of their thousand-dollar-a-night voices; I would rather boast that mine was the one free voice that could not be bought."

"There are no such vagrant, prodigal voices. A beautiful, trained voice is one of the highest products of civilization. It takes the most civilized listeners to appreciate it. It needs the stimulus of refined appreciation. It needs the inspiration of other voices and the spur of intelligent criticism. I know you have been making fun of my ambitions, but I choose to take you seriously. My standard would come down to the level of my audiences — the cowboys and the children in bed-quilts."

"Oh, no, it would n't. Your genius is its own standard, is it not? You would be like the early poets and the troubadours. They sang in rather an empty world, did

they not, and not always to critical audiences? The knights and barons could n't
have been much above our cowboys."

"Oh, how absurd you are! No, not absurd, but unkind; you are making desperate fun of me and of my voice too, because
I make so much of it — but you force me
to. It is my whole argument."

"I 'm desperate enough for anything, but
I 'm hardly in a position to make fun of my
rival. Madeline, sometimes I hate your
voice, and yet I love it too. I understand
its power better than you think. It has just
the dramatic quality which should make you
the singer of a new people. Oh, how blind
you are to a career so much finer, so much
broader, so much sweeter, and more womanly! Your mission is here, in the camps
of the Philistines. You are to bring a message to the heathen; to sing to the wandering, godless peoples, — to the Esaus and the
Ishmaels of the Far West."

"That is all very fine, but you know perfectly well that your Esaus and your Ishmaels would prefer a good clog-dancer to all
the ' messages ' in the world."

"Oh, you don't know them, — and if

they did, it would be the first part of your mission to teach them a higher sort of pleasure."

"And I am to go to Munich and study for the sake of coming out here to regenerate the cowboys?"

"That is n't the part of your destiny *I* insist upon," Aldis said, letting the weariness of discouragement show in his tones. "But you say you must have an audience. And I must have you"—

"But does it occur to you," Madeline interrupted quickly, "what a tremendous waste of effort and elaboration there would be between the means and the effect?"

"I don't ask for the effort and the elaboration. That is the part *you* insist upon. All I want is you, just as you are, voice or no voice. You need not go to Munich on my account."

"You expect me to give up everything."

"You would have to give up a good deal; I don't deny it. But is there any virtue in woman that becomes her better?"

"Perhaps not, from a man's point of view. But it is no use listening to you. You have n't the faintest conception of what

my future is to me, as I see it, and all this
you have been talking is either a burlesque
on my ambition, or else it is the insanity of
selfishness — masculine selfishness. I don't
mean anything personal. You want to absorb into your own life a thing that was
meant to have a life of its own, for all the
world to share and enjoy. Yes, why not?
I won't pretend to depreciate my gift! I am
only the tenement in which a precious thing
is lodged. You would drive out the divine
tenant, or imprison it, for the sake of pos-
sessing the poor house it lives in."

"Good Heavens!" Aldis exclaimed, with
a sort of awe of what seemed to him an
almost blasphemous absurdity. "What nonsense you young geniuses can talk! I wish
the precious tenant would evacuate and leave
you to your sober senses, and to me."

"And this is what a man calls love!"

Aldis laughed fiercely. "Has there been
any new kind of love invented lately? This
is the kind that came into the world before
art did."

"Art is love, without its selfishness," said
Madeline, with innocent conclusiveness.

"Where the deuce do you girls learn this

sort of talk?" Aldis demanded of the girl
beside him.

She answered him with unexpected gentleness. She leaned towards him, and looked
entreatingly in his face. "This is our last
evening together. Don't let us spoil it with
this wretched squabbling."

"She calls it squabbling — a man's fight
for his life!" He turned and gave her back
her look, with more fire than entreaty in his
eyes.

"There is the moon," she said hurriedly.
"It is time to go home."

The fringe of grasses above their heads
was touched with silver light, and the
shadow of the bluff lay broad and distinct
across the valley.

"We must go home," Madeline urged.
Aldis did not move.

"Madeline, would you marry me if I had
a lot of money?"

"Oh, hush!"

"No, but would you? Answer me."

"Yes, I would." She was tired of choos-
ing her words. "For then you would not
have to earn a living in these wild places."

"You would take me then as a sort of

appendage ? You don't want a man with work of his own to do ? "

" Not if it interferes with mine."

" That is your answer ? "

" Can I make it any plainer ? "

" You have not said you do not love me."

" I don't need to say it. It is proved by what I do — I might have been nicer to you, perhaps, but you are so unreasonable."

" Never mind if I am. Be nice to me now ! "

" I meant to be. But it is too late. We must go home." She felt that she was losing command of herself through sheer exhaustion ; any hint of weakness or hesitation now could only mislead him and prolong the struggle. " Come," she said, " you will have to get up first."

He did not move.

" Oh, sit still a little longer," he pleaded. " I will not bother you any more. Let us have one half hour of our old times together — only a little better, because it is the last."

" No, not another minute." She rose quickly to her feet, tripped in her skirt, and

tottered forward.   Aldis had risen too.   As
she reeled and threw out her hands, he
sprang between her and the brink, thrusting
her back with the whole force of his sudden
spring.   The rock upon which he had leaped
regardless of his footing gave its final quake
and dropped into the abyss.   It was the up-
permost segment of a loosened column.   The
whole mass went down, narrowing the ledge
so that Madeline, by turning her head, could
look into the depths below.   She did not
move or cry; she lay still, but for the deep
gasping breaths that would not cease, though
all the life had seemed to go out from her
when he went down.   The relief of unconsciousness did not come to her.   She was
aware of the soft, dry night wind growing
cool, of the river's soughing, of the long
grasses fluttering wildly against the moon
above her head.   The perfume of wild syringa blossoms, hidden in some crevice of the
rock, came to her with the breeze.   There
were crackling, rustling noises from the
depth of shadow, into which she dared not
look; then silence, except the wind and the
river's roar, borne strongly upwards, as it
freshened.   And all the words they had said

to each other in their long, passionate argument kept repeating themselves, forcing themselves upon her stunned, passive consciousness, she lying there, not caring if she never stirred again, and he on the rocks below; and between them the sudden, awful silence. She might have crept to the brink and called, but she could not call to the dead.

Gradually it came to her that she must get herself back somehow to the camp with her miserable story. It would be easier, it seemed, to turn once over and drop off the cliff, and let some one else tell the story for them both. But the fascination of this impulse could not prevail over the awakening shuddering fact of her physical being. She despised herself for the caution with which she crept along the ledge and up the grass-grown crevice. If he had been cautious she would be where he was lying now. It was her own rash girl's fancy for getting on the brink of things and looking over, that had brought them first to that fatal place. But these thoughts were but pin-pricks following the shock of that benumbing horror she was carrying with her back to the camp.

As she looked down upon its lights she felt like one already long estranged from the life of which she had been the gay centre but two hours before. She knew how her sister's little girls were asleep, the night wind softly stirring the leaves outside their bedroom window; how still the house was; how empty and white in the moonlight the tents on the hill; how the camp was assembled on the beach, waiting for her return with Aldis and for the evening singing. Sing! She could have shrieked, sobbed, and cried aloud at the thought of this home-coming — she alone with the burden of her sorrow, and by and by Aldis, borne in his comrades' arms and laid on his bed in that empty tent on the hill.

But there was a hard constriction, a dumb, convulsive ache in her throat. She felt as if no sound could ever be uttered by her again.

If Aldis had been lying dead at the foot of the bluffs, as Madeline believed, this story would never have been told in print, except in a cold-blooded newspaper paragraph, which would have omitted to mention one curious fact connected with the accident; that a

young girl, who was the companion of the
unfortunate young man when it occurred,
suffered a shock of the nerves from the sight
of his fall that deprived her entirely of her
voice, so that she could not speak except in
whispers.

It was not Aldis who was the victim of
this tragedy of the bluffs, but Aldis's successful rival, the Voice. It was hushed, at
the very moment of its triumph. A blow
from the brain upon those nerve - chords
which were its life — love shook the house
in which music dwelt, jarred it to its centre,
and the imperious but frail tenant had fled.

At the moment when Madeline's tortured
fancy was bringing him home a mangled
heap, and laying him in the last of that row
of tents on the hill, Aldis was getting himself home by the lower trail, as fast as his
bruises would let him.

He had fallen into a scrubby growth of
wild syringa, which flung its wax-white blossoms out from a cranny in the cliff, less than
half-way down. As he crashed into it, its
tough and springy mass checked his fall
enough to enable him to get a firm grasp
with his hands. He hung dangling at arm's

length against the cliff, groping for a tem-
porary lodgment for his feet. In the darkness he dimly perceived something like a
ledge, not too far below him, towards which
the face of the bluff sloped slightly out-
wards.

Flattening himself against the rock he let
go his hold and slid, clutching and grinding
downward, till his feet struck the ledge.
From this vantage, after getting his breath
and taking a deliberate view of his situation,
it was not a difficult feat to reach the slope
of broken rock below. He sat there while the
trembling in his strained muscles subsided,
scarcely conscious as yet of his torn and
scratched and bruised condition. He was
about to raise his voice in a shout to assure
Madeline of his safety, when the thought
turned him sick that, unnerved as she must
be with the sight of his fall, she might mistake the call for a cry for help, and venture
too near that treacherous edge to look down.
He kept still, while the horror grew upon
him of what might happen to Madeline
alone on the ledge, or trying to climb the
slippery crevice in the shadow of the bluff.
He knew that a mass of rock had fallen

when he fell; was there space enough left on the ledge by which she could safely reach the crevice? He could not resist giving one low call, speaking her name as distinctly and quietly as he could, and bidding her not move but listen. There was no answer; the roar of the rapids, borne on the wind that nightly drew down the cañon, drowned his voice. Madeline did not hear him. He waited until the silence convinced him that she was no longer there; then he took his way toilsomely back to the camp.

A light showed in the window of the office, which in the evening was usually dark. He found the family assembled there in the light of a single kerosene lamp, the flame of which was streaming up the chimney unobserved, while all eyes were bent upon Madeline, seated in one of the revolving office chairs, with her back to the desk. She leaned, shivering and whispering, towards her sister, who knelt on the floor before her, holding her hands and staring with a fearful interest into the girl's colorless face.

The men who stood nearest the door turned and started as Aldis entered.

" Why, good God, Aldis ! " Mr. Duncan
exclaimed. " Why, man, we thought you
were dead. You don't mean to say it 's you
— all of you ? "

" I 'm all here," said Aldis.

" He 's all here, Madeline," Mrs. Duncan
shouted hysterically to the girl, as if she
were deaf as well as dumb.

The fateful voice was undoubtedly gone.
Madeline could no longer plead a higher call
when the common destiny of woman was
offered her. But if Aldis had thought to
profit immediately by her release from the
claims of art, he was disappointed.

What was the new obstacle ? Only some
more of Madeline's high-flown nonsense, as
her sister called it. She was always making a heroic situation out of everything that
happened to her, and expecting her friends
to bear her out in it.

On the night of the adventure on the cliff
she had been put to bed, shaking with a nervous chill. Next day's packing had been
suspended, and the eastward journey post-
poned. But in a day or two she was sufficiently recovered to be walking again with

Aldis on the shore, and the old argument was resumed on a new basis. Madeline, pale and wistful, with Aldis's head very close to hers, that the river's intruding roar might not drown her whispers, protesting — sometimes with sobs, sometimes with sudden, tremulous laughter that shook her with dumb convulsions hardly more mirthful than the sobs — that she could not and she would not burden his life with the wreck she now passionately proclaimed herself to be.

But would she not give him what he wanted, had wanted, should continue to want and to try for so long as they both should live?

No, he did n't — he could n't possibly want a ridiculous muttering shadow of a woman beside him all the days of his life. It was only his magnanimity. She wondered he could believe her capable of the meanness of taking advantage of it.

Aldis did not despair, but it was certainly difficult, with happiness almost within his reach, with the girl herself sometimes sobbing in his arms, to be obliged to treat this obstacle as seriously as Madeline insisted it should be treated. He appealed to Mrs.

Duncan, who scolded and laughed at her
sister alternately, and quoted with elaborate
particulars a surprising number of similar
cases of voices lost and found again by
means of care and skillful treatment. But
hers was *not* a similar case, Madeline vehe-
mently declared. It was *not* from a cold,
like Mrs. So and So's ; it had not come on
gradually, beginning with a hoarseness, like
some one's else. It was — the girl believed
in her heart that she had been made a singular and impressive example of the folly
and wickedness of pride in an exceptional
gift, and of triumph in its corresponding destiny. The spirit she had boasted of harboring had deserted her. She deserved her
punishment, but she would not permit another's life to be shadowed by it, especially
one so generous — who, so far from resenting her refusal of the whole loaf, was content, or pretended to be, with the broken and
rejected fragments. But all this Madeline
was careful to keep from the cheerful irrev-
erence of her sister's comments. She faltered something like it to Aldis in one of
their long talks by the river ; his low tones
answering briefly and at long intervals her

piercing whispers, that sometimes almost shrieked her trouble in his ear. He could feel that she was still thrilling with the double shock she had suffered. He was infinitely tender with her, and patient with her extravagant expositions of the situation between them. He longed to heap savage ridicule upon them, but he forbore. He listened and waited and let her talk until she was worn out, and then they were happiest together. For a few moments each day it seemed that she might drift back to him on the ebb of that overstrained tide of resistance, and be at rest.

Madeline was always impatient of any discussion of the chances of her recovery; but one day, just before the time of their parting, Aldis surprised and captured an admission from her that there might be such a chance. Would she then, on the strength of that possibility, consent to be engaged to him and treat him as her accepted lover, since nothing but her pride now kept them apart?

"Pride," Madeline repeated; "I don't know what I have left to be proud of."

"There is a kind of stiff-necked humility

that is worse than pride," said Aldis, smiling at the easy way in which she shirked the logic of the conclusion he was forcing upon her. "You won't consent to the meanness, as you call it, of giving me what you are pleased to consider a damaged article, a thing with a flaw in it; as if a woman would be more lovable if she were proof against all wear and tear. But if the flaw can be healed, if there is a possibility that the voice may come back, why should we not be engaged on that hope?"

"And if it never does, will you promise to let me release you?"

"You can release me at any time — now, if you like."

"But will you promise to take your release when I give it to you?"

"We will see about that. Perhaps by the time your voice does n't come back I shall have been able to make you believe that it is n't the voice I care for."

"And if it should come back," cried Madeline with sudden enthusiasm, "I shall have my triumph! I am done forever with all that nonsense about Art and Destiny. If my voice ever does come back, I shall not let it bully me. It shall not decide my fate. You will see. Oh, how I wish you *might* see! I have learned my lesson in the true, awful values of things. Thank Heaven it has cost no more! There is one less singer in the world, perhaps, but there is not one less life. Your life. If you had lost it that night, and I had kept my voice, do you think I should ever have had any joy in it again — ever lifted it up, as I boasted to you I would some day, before crowds of listeners? Could I have gone before the footlights, bowing and smiling, with my arms full of flowers, and remembered your face and your last look as you went down?"

"Then it is settled at last, voice or no voice?"

"Yes, — but I am so sorry for you! It will not come back; I know it never will, and I shall go on whispering and gibbering to the end of my days, and all your friends will pity you; it is such a painfully conspicuous thing!"

"I want to be pitied. I am just pining to be an object of general compassion. Only I want to choose what I shall be pitied for."

" Choose ? " said Madeline stupidly.
" What *do* you mean ? "

" Have I not chosen? Now be as sorry
for me as you like. And we 'll ask for the
sympathy of the camp to-night. It will be
a blow to the boys — my throwing myself
away like this ! "

" How ridiculous you are ! " sighed Madeline. It was a luxury, after all, to yield.
And perhaps in the depths of her consciousness, bruised and quivering as it was, there
lingered a faint image of herself, as a charming girl sees herself reflected in those flatter-
ing mirrors, the eyes of friends, kindred,
and adorers. Voiceless, futureless, spoiled
as was the budding prima donna, the girl
remained: eighteen years old and fair to
look upon, with perfect health, and all the
mysterious, fitful, but unquenchable joy of
youth thrilling through her pulses. Perhaps in the innocent joy of her own intentions towards him, she was not so sorry for
Aldis after all. The sobs, the frantic whispers died away, and were hushed in a blissful acquiescence. She was not less fascinating to her lover — half amazed at his own
sudden triumph — in her blushing, starry-

eyed silences, than she had been in all the eager redundance of her lost utterance. That was a wonderful last day for the young man to dream over, in the long months before they should meet again!

The camp had moved out of the cañon and down upon the desert plains. It was an open winter. Up to the first of January the contractors had been able to keep their men at work, following closely the locating party.

Aldis rode up and down the line, putting in fresh stakes for the contractors, keeping them true to the line, and watching incidentally that they did not pad their embankments with sage-brush. His summer camp-dress of broad-shouldered, breezy, flannel shirt, and slender-waisted trousers, was changed to a reefing-jacket, double-buttoned to the chin, long boots, and helmet-shaped cap, pulled low down to keep the wind out of his eyes. Strong wintry reds and browns replaced, on his thin cheek, the summer's pallor.

Madeline Hendrie, dressing for dinner at the Sutherland in New York, where she and her sister were spending the winter, stood

before her toilet-glass fastening her laces,
her eyes fixed alternately on her own reflec-
tion in the mirror and on a dim photograph
that leaned against the frame. It was not a
bad specimen of amateur photography. It
represented a young man on horseback in
a wide and windy country, with an expression
of sadness and determination in the dark
eyes that looked steadfastly out of the gray,
toneless picture.

They were the most beautiful eyes in
the world, Madeline thought to herself; and
sinking on her knees before the low table,
with her arms crossed on the lace, rose-lined
cover, she would brood in a fond, luxurious
melancholy over the picture — over the som-
bre line of plain and distant mountain and
the chilly little cluster of tents, huddled
close together by the river's dark, swift
flood flowing between icy beaches, below
barren shores, where a few leafless willows
shivered and the wild-twisted clumps of sage
defied the cold.

A moment later she was rustling softly
down the corridor at her sister's side, passing groups of ladies who looked after them
with that comprehensive but impersonal

scrutiny which is a woman's recognition of anything unusual in another's dress or appearance. Mrs. Duncan looked her sister over with a quick, intelligent side glance, for those silent eye comments were all turned upon Madeline. She could see nothing amiss with the girl; she was looking very lovely, a trifle absent. Madeline had a way lately of looking as if she were alone with her own thoughts, on occasions when other women's faces took on habitually a neutral and impassive expression. It made her conspicuous, as if hers were the only sensitive human countenance exposed in a roomful of masks.

"Why do you never wear your light dresses, Madeline?" said Mrs. Duncan, with the intention of rousing the girl from her untimely dream. "You are very effective in black, with your hair, but I should think you would like once in a while to vary the effect."

"Do you suppose I am studying effects for the benefit of these people? I am saving my light dresses."

"Saving them! What for?"

"Do you never save up a pretty dress that Will likes, when you are away from him?"

" No, indeed I don't. It would get out of style, and he would see there was something wrong with it, though he might not know what it was. Dresses won't keep! Besides, do you think you are never to have any new ones, now you are engaged to an engineer?"

"I shall not need many if I go West, and a year or two behind won't matter to — my engineer!"

" Oh, you poor innocent! You don't know your engineer yet; and you don't know your West, either. And one is always having to pack up and come East at short notice, and I know of nothing more insupportable than to find one's self dumped off an overland train in New York in the middle of winter, for instance, with a veteran outfit one has n't had the strength of mind to 'give to the poor,' as Will says. You never know how your clothes look till you have packed them up on one side of the continent and unpacked them on the other. And let me tell you it pays to dress well in camp. Nothing is too good for them, poor things, so long as it 's not inappropriate. Do you suppose a man ever forgets how a

woman ought to look? Wear out your
things, my dear, and take the good of them
before they get *passé*, and let the future take
care of itself."

Madeline was laughing, and the dreamy
soft abstraction had vanished. A stranger
might look into her liquid, half-averted eyes,
and see no more there than was meant for
the passing glance.

Aldis had the promise of a month's leave
of absence in March, but soon after the 1st
of January the weather turned suddenly cold.
The contractors took their men off the work,
and the time of Aldis's leave was thus anticipated by two months. He telegraphed to
Mrs. Duncan that he would be in New York
by the 15th, allowing for all contingencies.

Madeline's joy over the telegram was increased by one small item, of relief from the
necessity of delaying a communication which
she dreaded making by letter. With rest
and skillful treatment her voice had come
back, as her sister had prophesied, in its full
compass and purity. Her musical instructor
had urged her to try it once upon an audience, in a not too conspicuous rôle, before
she went abroad to study ; for Madeline had

not yet found courage to confess her apostasy.

The temptation to sing once as she had so often dreamed of singing, with the support of a magnificent orchestra; the longing to know just how much she was resigning in turning her back upon a musical career, were overmastering.

Moreover, her music was the sole dowry with which she could enrich her husband's life. She had a curious, persistent humility about herself, apart from the gift which she had grown to consider the essential quality of her being. She desired intensely to know just how much it was in her power to endow her lover with, over and above what his generosity, as she insisted upon calling it, demanded. For Madeline did nothing by halves. She could abandon herself to a passion of surrender as completely as she had done to the fire of resistance; and while she was about it, she wished to feel that it was no paltry thing she was giving up. But she was wise enough in her love to reflect that possibly Aldis might not be able fully to enter into the joy of her magnificent renunciation. There might be a pang, an uneasiness to him, so far away from her, in the thought that his old enemy was again in the field. So Aldis only knew this much of her recovery, that she could speak once more in her natural voice. She would reserve her triumph, if so it should prove, until his home-coming, when she could lay it at his feet with a joyous humility and such assurances of her love as no letter could convey.

On the 13th of January she was to be the soloist at a popular concert to be given that evening; one of a series where the character of the music and of the audience was exceedingly good, and the orchestral support all that a singer's heart could desire. On the 15th Aldis would come home.

It was all delightfully dramatic; and Madeline was not yet so in love with obscurity as to be quite indifferent to the scenic element in life.

In his telegram Aldis had allowed for a two days' delay on business at Denver. Arriving at that city, however, he found that, in the absence of one of the principal parties concerned, his business would have to be deferred. He was therefore due in New York on the 13th. He had not telegraphed again

to his Eastern friends; it had seemed like
making too much of a ceremony of his home-
coming.   He dropped off the train from the
North at the Grand Central Depot in the
white early dusk of a snowy afternoon,
when the quiet up-town streets were echoing
to the sound of snow-shovels, and the muffled
tinkle of car-bells came at long intervals
from the neighboring avenues.   He hurried
ahead of the long line of passengers, jumped
on the rear platform of a crowded car that was
just moving off, and in twenty minutes was
at his hotel.   He tried to master his great
but tremulous joy, to dine deliberately, to
do his best for his outer man, before pre-
senting himself to Madeline; but his lonely
fancy had dwelt so long and with such intensity on this meeting that now he was
almost unnerved by the nearness of the
reality.

The reality was after all only a neat maid,
who said, as he offered his card at the door
of Mrs. Duncan's apartment, that the ladies
were both out.   It was impossible to accept
the statement simply and go away.   Were
the ladies out for the evening? he asked.
Yes, they had gone to a concert or the opera,

or something, at the Academy of Music. Mrs. Duncan always left word where she was going when she and Miss Madeline both went out, on account of the children. The maid looked at him with intelligent friendliness. She was perfectly aware of the significance of the name on the card she held. She waited while Aldis scribbled a few words on another card which he asked her to give to Mrs. Duncan when the ladies returned, in case he should miss them at the concert. In the street he debated briefly whether to endure a few more hours of waiting, or hasten on to the mixed joy of a meeting in a crowd. Yet such meetings were not always infelicitous. Delicious moments of isolation might come to two in a great assembly, hushed, driven together in a storm of music. There seemed a peculiar fascinating fitness in the situation. Music, which had threatened to part them, should, like a hireling, celebrate their reunion.

The violins were in full cry, behind the green baize doors, mingling with the clear, terse notes of a piano, as he passed into the lobby of the Academy. While he waited for the concerto to end, his eyes rested me-

chanically upon the portraits of prima don-
nas, whose names were new to him, in smiles
and low corsages and wonderful coiffures of
the latest fashion ; and he said to himself that
well it was for those fair dames, but not for
his ladye — his little girl, she was safe among
the listeners, unknown, unpublished. *For*
her, not *of* her, the loud instruments were
speaking, in that vast, hushed, resounding
temple of music.

He would see her first with her rapt face
turned towards the stage. He would know
her by the outline of her cheek, her little
ear, and the soft light tangle of curls hiding
her temples. She would not be exalted
above him in the Olympian circle of the
boxes ; she would be in the balcony, not in
full-dress, but with some marvel of a little
bonnet framing the color and light and
sweetness of her face. Her cloak would
have slipped down from her smooth, silken
sleeves and shoulders. In his restless, waiting dream, while the music sank and swelled
in endless cadences behind the barriers, he
could see her with distracting vividness : her
listening attitude, her lifted, half-averted
face, her slender passive hands in her lap,

her soft, deep, joyous breathing stirring the lace or ribbons at her throat.

He was prepared to find her very dainty and unapproachably elegant; there had been a hint of such formidable but delightful possibilities in the cut of her simple camp dresses and in the way she wore them. He glanced disconsolately at his own modestly dressed person, with which he was so monotonously familiar, and wondered if Madeline would find him " Western."

The concerto was over at last. He passed down the aisle and along the rear wall of the balcony, keeping under the shadow of the first tier of boxes, while he took a survey of the house. It seemed bewilderingly brilliant to Aldis, seeing it in a setting of frontier life for the first time in three years; a much more complex emotion to one born to the life around him, and estranged from it, than to him who sees it for the first time as a spectacle in which he has never had a part. It was with rather a heart-sick gaze he searched the rows and rows of laughing women's faces, banked like flowers against the crimson and white and gold of the partitions.

Suddenly the murmur pervading the house sank into an expectant silence — the musicians' chairs were filling up; but only the grayheaded first violins were leaning to their instruments and fingering their music. The leader's music-stand had been moved aside to make room for the soloist, a young débutante, so the whispers around him announced, who was now coming forward, winding her silken train past the musicians' stands, her hand in that of the leader. Now she sank before the hushed crowd, dedicating to it, as it were, herself, her beauty, her song, her whole blissful young presence there.

Aldis crushed the unfolded programme he held in his hand. He did not need to consult it for the name of the fair young candidate. The blood rushed into his face, and then left it deadly white. His heart was pounding with a raging excitement, but he did not move or take his eyes from Madeline's face. She stood, faintly smiling down upon the crowd, folding and unfolding the music in her hands, while the orchestra played the prelude. Then on the deepening silence came the first notes of her voice.

Aldis had never imagined anything like the
pang of delicious pain it gave him. Its personality pierced his very soul. Every word
of the recitative, in the singer's pure enun-
ciation, could be heard. The song was
Heine's " Lorelei,"·with Liszt's music, and
the orchestration was worthy of the music.

" I know not what it presages," — the
recitative began, — " this heart with sadness fraught." Aldis took a deep, hard
breath. He knew the story that was coming. The rocks, the river, the evening sky
— he knew them all. Had she forgotten?
Did the great god Music deprive a woman
of her memory, her tender womanly com-
punction, as well as her heart? Was this
beautiful creature, with eyes alight and soft
throat swelling to the notes of her song,
merely a voice, after all, celebrating its own
triumph and another's allurement and despair? Was the heart that beat under the
laces that covered that white bosom merely
a subtle machine for setting free those wonderful sounds that floated down to him and
seemed to bid him farewell?

Now, in a wild crescendo, with a hurry of
chords in the accompaniment, the end has

come; the boat and man are lost. Then
an interlude, and the pure, pitiless voice
again, lamenting now, not triumphing —
"And this, with her magic singing, the
Lorelei hath done — the Lorelei hath done."
The song died away and ceased in mourn-
ful repetitions, and the audience gave itself
up to a transport of applause. It had won
— a new singer; and he had lost — only his
wife. He stood there, unknown and unheeded, a pitiful minority of one, and accepted his defeat.

The frantic clappings continued. They
were demanding an encore. The friendly
old fellows in the orchestra were looking back
across the stage to welcome the singer's return. They had assisted at the triumph of
so many young aspirants and queens of the
hour. This one was coming back, flushed
and smiling, her face beautiful in its new
joy, as she sank down again with her arms
full of flowers, gratefully, submissively, before the audience at whose command she was
there. The great house was enchanted with
her and with its own unexpected enthusiasm.
A joyous thrill and murmur, the very breath
of that adulation which is dearest to the

goddess of the foot-lights, floated up to the intoxicated girl, wrapt in the wonder of her own success. Aldis could bear no more. He made his way out, pursued by the furious clappings, by the silence, by the first thrilling notes of the encore. He walked the streets for hours, then went to his room, and threw himself, face downward, on his bed. The lace curtains of his window let in a pallid glimmer from the electric lights in the square, — a ghastly fiction of a moon that never waxes nor wanes. The night spent itself, the tardy winter morning crept slowly over the city and wrapt it in chill sea fog.

Mrs. Duncan woke with a hoarse feverish cold, and wished that she had given Aldis's card and message to Madeline the night before. She had kept them from her, sure that they would rob the excited girl of what was left of her night's sleep. Now she felt too ill to make the disclosure and face Madeline's alarm. She waited, with cowardly procrastination, until the late breakfast was over and her little girls had been hurried off to school. She and Madeline had drawn their chairs close to the soft coal fire to talk over the concert, Madeline with a heap of morning papers in her lap, through which she was looking for the musical notices, when Mrs. Duncan gave her Aldis's note. It required no explanation or comment. It said that he hoped to find them at the Academy of Music, but if he failed to do so, this was to prepare them for an early call; he was coming as early as he could hope to see them, — nine o'clock, he suggested, with insistence that made itself felt even in the careless words of the note. It was now nearly ten o'clock; he had not come. The gray morning turned a sickly yellow and the streets looked wet and dirty. The papers were tossed into a corner of the sofa, where Mrs. Duncan had taken refuge from Madeline's restless wanderings about the room.

A mass of hot-house roses, trophies of the evening's triumph, were displayed on the closed piano, shedding their languid sweetness unheeded; except once when Madeline stopped near them, and exclaimed to her sister : —

" Oh, do tell Alice to take those flowers away ! " and the next moment seemed to forget they were still there.

The ladies breakfasted and lunched in

their own rooms, dining only in the restaurant below. When lunch was announced, Mrs. Duncan rose from her heap of shawls and sofa-cushions and went to the window, where Madeline stood gazing out into the yellow mist that hid the square.

"Come, girlie, come out and keep me company. A watched pot never boils, you know."

"Do you *want* any lunch?" Madeline asked incredulously.

Mrs. Duncan did not want any, but she was willing to pretend that she did for the sake of interrupting the girl's unhappy watch.

The two women sat down opposite each other in the little dark dining-room, the one window of which looked into a dingy well inclosed by the many-storied walls of the house. The gas was burning, but enough gray daylight mingled with it to give a sickly paleness to the faces it illumined.

There was a letter lying by Madeline's plate.

"When did this come?" she demanded of Alice, the maid.

"They sent it up, miss, with the lunch-tray."

"Oh!" cried Madeline. "It may have been lying there in the office for hours!"

She read a few words of the letter, got up from the table, and left the room. Mrs. Duncan gave her a few moments to herself, and then followed her. She was in the parlor, turning over the heap of papers in a distracted search for something which she could not seem to find.

"Oh, Sallie," she exclaimed, looking up piteously at her sister, "won't you find when the Boston Shore line train goes out? I think it is two o'clock, and it's after one now."

"Why do you want to know about the Boston trains?"

"Read that letter — I'm going to try to see him before he starts — read the letter!" she repeated, in answer to her sister's amazed expostulatory stare. She ran out of the room while Mrs. Duncan was reading the letter, and in her own chamber tore off her wrapper and began dressing for the street. Mrs. Duncan heard bureau-drawers flying open and hurried footsteps as she read. This was Aldis's letter : —

Wednesday morning.

DEAR MADELINE,— I saw you at the Academy last night when the verdict was given that separates us.

The destiny I would not believe in has become a reality to me at last. I must stand aside, and let it fulfill itself.

Last night I accused you of bitter things — you can imagine what, seeing you so, without any forewarning; but I am tolerably sane this morning. I know that nothing of all that maddened me is true, except that I love you and must give you back to your fate that claims you. You were never mine except by default.

I am going on to Boston this afternoon. I cannot trust myself to see you. I could not bear your compassion or your remorse, and if you were to offer me more than that, God knows what sacrifice I might not be base enough to accept, face to face with you again.

Good-by, my dearest, my only one. I think nothing can ever hurt me much after this. But do not grieve over what neither of us could have helped. The happiness of one man should not stand in the way of the free exercise of a divine gift like yours, and the memory of our summer in the cañon — of our last days there together, when my soul set itself to the music of those silences between us — that is still mine. Nothing can take that from me. Yours always.

Hugh Aldis.

" Madeline, you are not going after him ! " Mrs. Duncan protested, looking up from the letter with tears in her eyes, as her sister entered the parlor, in cloak and bonnet.

Madeline heard the protest ; she did not see the tears.

" Don't *talk* to me, — help me, Sallie ! Can't you see what I have done ? Find me that Boston train, won't you ? I know there is one in the evening, but he said afternoon. Where *is* it ? " she wailed, turning over with trembling hands sheet after sheet of bewildering columns which mocked her with advertisements of musical entertainments, and even with her own name staring at her in print.

" The *train* goes at two o'clock, but you shall not go racing up there after him, you crazy girl ! I 'd go myself, only I 'm too sick. I 'm awfully sorry for him, but he 'll come back — they always do — and give you a chance to explain."

" Explain ! I 'm going to see him for one

instant if I can. I 've got just twenty minutes, and nothing on earth shall stop me ! "

" Alice," Mrs. Duncan called down the
passage, as Madeline shut the outer door,
" put on your things and go after Miss Madeline, quick — Third Avenue Elevated to
the Grand Central. You 'll catch her if you
hurry, before she gets up the steps."

Mistress and maid reached the Grand
Central station together, a few minutes before the train moved out. The last of the
line of passengers, ticket in hand, were filing
past the door-keeper. It needed but a glance
to assure Madeline that Aldis was not among
them. It would be safer, she decided
quickly, to get out upon the platform in
broadside view from the windows of the
train. If Aldis were already on the train,
or, better still, on the platform, and should
see her, Madeline felt sure he would instantly know why she was there.

" I only want to see a friend who is going
by the Boston train," she said to the door-
keeper. " I 'm not going myself." He hesitated, and said something about his orders.
" If I must have a ticket, my maid will get
me one, but I cannot wait ; you must let

me through!" She handed her purse to Alice. The man at the gate said he guessed it was no matter about a ticket. He looked curiously after her as she sped along the platform — such a pretty girl, her cheeks red and her hair all out of crimp with the dampness, but with a sob in her voice and eyes strained wide with trouble!

"Last train down on the right!" he called after her. "You'll have to hurry." Ominous clouds of steam were puffing out of a smoke-stack far ahead of her; men were swinging themselves aboard from the platform where they had been walking up and down.

"Boston Shore line, miss?" a porter lounging by his empty truck called to Madeline as she came panting up to the rear car.

"Oh, yes!" she sobbed. "Is it gone?"

The train gave one heavy, clanking lurch forward. The porter laughed, caught her by the arms, and swung her lightly up to the platform of the last car. The brakeman seized her and shunted her in at the door. The train was in motion. She clung wildly to the door-handle a moment, looking back, and then sank into the nearest seat and burst into tears. Curious glances were cast at her from the neighboring seats, but Madeline was oblivious of everything but the grotesque misery of her situation. What would Alice think, and what would poor, frantic Sallie think, what even would the man at the gate think, who had taken her word instead of a ticket! The conductor came round after a while, and Madeline appealed to him. She had been put on the train by mistake. She had no money and no ticket, but there was, she thought, a friend of hers aboard — would the conductor kindly find out for her if a Mr. Aldis were in any of the forward cars, and tell him that a lady, a friend of his, wished to see him ?

The conductor had a broad, purple, smooth-shaven cheek, which overflowed his stiff shirt-collar; he stroked the tuft of coarse beard on the end of his chin, as he assured the young lady that she need not distress herself. He would find the gentleman if he were on the train. Was he a young gentleman, for instance ?

"Yes, he was young and tall, and had dark eyes " — Suddenly Madeline stopped and blushed furiously, meeting the conductor's small and merry eye fixed upon her in the abandonment of her trouble.

The door banged behind him. The car swayed and leaped on the track as the motion of the train increased. A long interval, then a loud crash of noise from the wheels as the door opened again at the forward end of the car. A gentleman was coming down the aisle, looking from side to side as if in search of some one.

Madeline squeezed herself back into the corner of her seat next the window. The blood dropped out of her hot cheeks and stifled her breathing. She turned away her face, and buried it in her muff as some one stopped at her seat, and said, leaning with one hand on the back of it, " Is this the lady who wished to see me ? "

Aldis's face was as white as her own. His hand gripped the seat to hide its shaking. Madeline swept back her skirts, and he took the seat beside her. A long silence. Madeline's cheek and profile emerged from the muff and became visible in rosy silhouette against the blank white mist outside the window. Her color had come back.

" Did you get my letter ? "

" Yes. That is what brought me here."

Another silence. Madeline slid the hand next to Aldis out of her muff. He took no notice of it at first, then suddenly his own closed over it, and crushed it hard.

" You must not go to Boston to-night," she whispered.

" Why not ? "

" Because I am in such trouble ! — I had to see you, after that letter. I ran after the train, and they caught hold of me and put me on before I knew what they were doing ; and here I am without a ticket or a cent of money — and all because you would not come and let me — tell you " — She had hidden her face again in her muff.

" Tell me — what ? " His head was close to hers, his arm against her shoulder. He could feel her long, shuddering sobs.

" How *could* I come ? " he said.

She did not answer. The roar and rattle of the train went sounding on. It was very interesting to the people in the car; but Madeline had forgotten them, and Aldis cared no more for the files of faces than if they had been the rocky fronts of the bluffs that had kept a summer's watch over him and the girl beside him, and the noise of the train had been the far-off river's roar. He was in a dream which could not last too long.

Madeline lifted her head, and through the lulling din he heard her voice saying : —

"Oh, the river ! I seemed to hear it last night when I was singing, and the light on the rocks — do you remember? And I was so glad the rest was not true. And then your letter came " —

"Never mind ; nothing is true — only this," he roused himself to say.

The crowded train went roaring and swaying on, as it had during all the days and nights of his journey home, mingling its monotone with the dream that was coming true at last.

Somewhere in that vague and rapidly lessening region known as the frontier, there disappeared, a few years ago, a woman's voice. A soprano with a wonderful mezzo quality, those who knew it called it, and the girl, besides her beauty, had quite a distinct promise of dramatic power. But, they added, she seemed to have no imagination, no conception of the value of her gifts. She threw away a charming career, just at its outset, and went West with a husband — not anybody in particular. It was altogether a great pity. Perhaps she had not the artistic temperament, or was too indolent to give the time and labor required for the perfecting of her rare gift — at all events the voice was lost.

But in the camps of engineers, within sound of unknown waters, on mountain trails, or crossing the windy cattle-ranges, or in the little churches of the valley towns, or at a lonely grave perhaps, where his comrades are burying some unwitting, unacknowledged hero, dead in the quiet doing of his duty, a voice is sometimes heard, in ballad or gay roulade, anthem or requiem, — a voice those who have heard it say they will never forget.

Lost it may be to the history of famous voices, but the treasured, self-prized gifts are not those that always carry a blessing with them; and the soul of music, wherever it is purely uttered, will find its listeners; though it be a voice singing in the wilderness, in the dawn of the day of art and beauty which is coming to a new country and a new people.